HIS LOVIN
AUTHORESS SECRET

HIS LOVING AIN'T FOR ME
AUTHORESS SECRET

AUTHORESS SECRET
His Loving Ain't For Me

Copyright © 2023 by Authoress Secret All rights reserved.

No part of this publication may be reproduced, distributed, or transmitted in any form or by any means, including photocopying, recording, or other electronic or mechanical methods, without the prior written permission of the publisher, except in the case of brief quotations embodied in critical reviews and certain other noncommercial uses permitted by copyright law.

ISBN: 9798389871342

To:

From:

Authoress Secret
His Loving Ain't For Me

Chapter 1
Ghora

"Nano is mine and I will cut you from head to toe about my nigga," Rhema screamed.

"Excuse me but are you talking to me?" I pressed her as I looked around.

There was no one around.

"Yes, bitch, I am talking to you. Are you deaf and dumb?" Rhema bellowed.

"Nano and I are just friends, so calm down little baby," I replied.

"I should cut your fuckin face." Rhema shrieked.

She had a razor in her hand.

I was walking towards the mall entrance when this deranged bitch confronted me about a nigga with community dick. What the fuck I looked like fuckin around with a broke ass nigga who fucks everybody? My pussy is very precious to me and I definitely don't get the fuck down like that.

"BITCH, ARE YOU CRAZY? I HOPE THAT YOU KNOW HOW TO USE THAT DAMN RAZOR BECAUSE YOU ARE NOT GOING TO DO SHIT TO ME! FUCK AROUND AND GET CUT THE FUCK UP WITH YOUR OWN SHIT!" I screeched.

"Ghera, if I catch you with Nano again all hell will break loose," Rhema warned me.

"Seriously, Rhema, I am shaking in my boots. Girl, bye because I am not thinking about you." I laughed in Rhema's face.

"I am not playing with you." Rhema retorted.

"Listen, sis, if you have a problem with me speaking with Nano then I suggest that you take all of this shit up with him. That's your man. I don't want or need your girlfriend. We are friends and that's all." I explained to Rhema.

"Yeah, yeah, yeah, that's what they all say." Rhema angrily spat.

"Yeah maybe they do but I am different. I am not your average chick. I am cut from a different cloth. Trust me when I say I am not fuckin your baby daddy. I don't want your man because his love ain't for me." I stated.

"What makes you so different from the rest?" Rhema rolled her eyes as she questioned me.

"I am not looking for a booty call, a baby daddy, or a one-night stand. I need a nigga that's going to match every fuckin thing that I bring to the table. Trust me, Nano doesn't meet those qualifications." I informed Rhema.

I hoped that this would calm her nerves some because she was really checking the wrong bitch.

"I don't know if I should believe you," Rhema said, giving me an unsure look.

"Rhema, why are you so insecure? Could it be that you know that Nano is a piece of shit?" I inquired.

Rhema glared at me.

"I know my baby daddy is running around with every whore in town." Rhema wailed.

"Rhema, why do you want to subject yourself and your child to a life of misery? You already know how Nano is and if his ass hasn't changed yet what makes you feel like he will change for you and the baby? The nigga is showing you his true feelings. Nano doesn't give two fucks about you. Move on baby girl." I advised.

"I want a family." Rhema sobbed.

"Chile, please. You can have a family without Nano. Go find somebody that loves all of you including your dirty draws. Don't waste your time on a fuck boy." I advised her.

"Ghera, you have given me something to think about. I am not happy with Nano.

Ever since I had London, he has been acting very distant. As if he has something or someone else on his mind." Rhema replied.

"Look, I am not trying to get in your business but don't be a damn fool for nobody. Fuck Nano." I advised Rhema because I did not like the way that Nano was out here making her look like a fool. Rhema is a good girl and didn't deserve to be broken the way that she was. Nano doesn't love himself so I know damn well he's just fuckin with Rhema's heart.

She's smart, witty, and absolutely gorgeous. Any nigga would be happy to make Rhema his wife.

"I hear what you are saying, Ghera. I am not a bit offended at all. I just need to figure this shit out because I am not feeling Nano the way that I used to. I mean look at me. I am out here acting crazy about a piece of shit that doesn't come home at night." I admitted.

"Dry your eyes, sweetie. The best thing that you ever did was admit that there is a problem. You deserve better. The sky's the limit." Ghera hugged me.

"Whew, chile. It feels good to get this stuff off my chest. It's liberating." I muttered.

"Baby, I have been where you are. I definitely understand. Some of these niggas ain't shit. Just be careful who you choose to fuck with because most of these knuckleheads are not being honest. All they see is a pretty face and a big ass. Most want to fuck up your life by pumping you up with babies that they don't tend to take care of. Rhema just gives yourself some self-love and takes care of London and I promise all that you ever dreamed of will fall into place." Ghera advised me.

CHAPTER 2
RHEMA

Ghera was right. I should just get rid of Nano because all he did was keep me upset. He wasn't doing shit to make this relationship better. Nano hasn't given me one legit reason to stay. Yes, the dick was good and the bills were paid but I spent way too many nights alone just crying my eyes out. Whenever I called Nano he didn't pick up my calls or answer my texts. No one is that busy especially when your phone is always at your side when he's here with me and the baby.

I needed to get off my ass and start running my own show because ain't nothing popping this way with Nano. After my confrontation with Ghera in the mall parking lot, I went to Kossi's house to pick up my daughter. I had a lot on my mind. I couldn't just up and leave Nano like Ghera was suggesting because I had no job.

The little savings that I did have was for diapers and baby stuff for my daughter London. I needed some money so the first thing in the morning I was going job hunting instead of catering to Nano. He didn't deserve any more of this good pussy anyway.

Kossi was sitting outside playing with London in her yard.

"It looks like I am about to interrupt a fun time." I laughed.

"No, ma'am, you came at the perfect time. I am ready for a hot bath with some Epsom salts added so I can go to bed. When I say Auntie Kossi is tired, baby, that's what I mean." Kossi giggled.

"I hear you loud and clear. I promise that I won't keep you from that wonderful bathtime." I retorted.

"Thank you, sweetheart, because auntie is ready to hit the sheets." Kossi laughed.

"Kossi, do you mind if I bring London earlier tomorrow? I want to go job hunting." I uttered.

"Rhema if there is anything that I can do to help you and this child believe me when I say I will do it. I will be waiting. Is everything alright, what do you need a job for?" Kossi questioned me with her hand on her neck.

"Nano and I aren't working out. He's messing around with other girls and I am sick of his shit. I just need money for my own place, auntie. I want to get away from that nigga so badly." I whimpered.

"Is it really that bad?" Kossi questioned me.

"Yes, if I call his phone right now he won't answer and if he does he will be on some funny shit like we're not together. But when he's home he acts like everything is okay. I am just over all of it." I revealed this to my auntie.

"Baby, you don't need no damn job to leave Nano's no good ass. Leave London here and go pack all of your shit and come back home where you belong. I have been taking care of you since your mother and father died in that plane crash when you were three years old. You are my baby girl and if you need to come back home then damn it the doors are open." Kossi rambled.

"Okay, Auntie, I won't be long. I know that you are ready to take your bath." I told her.

"I am going to take my bath and give it to Miss. London one too. Just handle your business, Rhema." Kossi hurried me away.

"Bye, mommy." London waved at me.

*

Kossi has always been my life savior. I still wanted to find a job because I didn't want to live off my Auntie especially now that I have London. I wanted to be independent but first I needed a job. I think that I should stay with Kossi until I have savings. I wondered what the job market was like.

My phone rang.

"Rhema, do you want to go out to eat with me and Alan?" Tika asked me.

"Sure, what time?" I asked Tika.

"Around 5," Tika uttered.

"I don't know if I will be done moving by then," I told her.

"Why are you moving? Did you and Nano find a better place?" Tika wondered.

"No, I am leaving Nano. I have had it with his ass." I spat.

"It's about time. You are too pretty and smart to be dealing with his constant bullshit." Tika was so proud of me.

"Thanks, best friend." I happily spat.

"I am heading over there to help you out. We can get this done faster together. I am at mom's house so I am just going to leave

Alan here with her for a few hours." Tika told me.

"I will see you there. I love you." I ended the call.

I pulled up to the apartment building and noticed Nano's truck. Damn. I didn't want any problems with him.

I went inside the house and all I heard was some bitch moaning. It sounds like fucking noises. I went back outside to call Tika but she had already pulled up.

"Why do you look so sad?" Tika questioned me.

I didn't answer. I dragged her into my apartment by her arm.

"What the fuck! Who is that?" Tika asked me.

The noises were getting louder and louder. Whoever this bitch was had to have been here before because she was a little bit too comfortable for my liking. I grabbed some cooking oil and headed for my bedroom. I opened the oil and just started pouring it on Nano and his bitch.

"Ohh, that's cold!" The whore yelped.

Pow!

Tika started banging the bitch with the broom.

"What the fuck are you doing?" Nano screamed with a look of bewilderment in his eyes.

"Ahhh, my fuckin head!" The bitch yelled.

"Jessica! Jessica, is that you?" I asked.

I couldn't believe it. My fuckin hairdresser was fuckin my man in my bed.

"Rhema, I can explain! I can explain!" Jessica jumped her naked ass from my king size bed.

I was so hurt and upset. Why did Nano have to fuck this slut in our bed?

I went crazy on Jessica's ass. I slapped, kicked, and punched her in every which way that I could. I was fuckin tired of all of this bullshit and she was the one who had to feel my wrath.

"I am going to destroy your reputation in this state. I am going to tell everyone how you fucked my man in my bed. You dirty ass slut!" I howled.

MY knuckles were bloody.

"Baby, stop it! You are going to kill her." Nano pulled Jessica from my grasp.

"That bitch deserves to be in her grave!" I snarled.

I watched as she snuck out the door.

Jessica was still bloody and butt ass naked. I saw her keys in her hand though.

"Yeah, you better run, bitch!" I opened up the window and shouted.

"Leave her alone, Rhema. You damn sure know how to fuck up a good nut! Fuck, man!" Nano groaned.

"Nigga, shut the fuck up! You are weird as a bitch!" I fumed as I helped Tika pack.

"What the fuck did you say, bitch?" Nano stepped into my face.

"Boy, bye! I got time for none of your shit that you are talking about. I said what I said and I ain't changing it." I blurted not giving a fuck.

I was tired of Nano and all of his bullshit.

"You need your ass whipped, huh? Are you trying to be tough, huh, bitch?" Nano breathed his shitty ass breath into my face.

"Nigga, get the fuck out of my niece's face before I blow your motherfucking brains out! " Uncle Bruno bellowed.

"Rhema just beat the brakes off Nano's bitch that we caught him in here fuckin in the bed." Tika quickly told Uncle Bruno.

"Motherfucker, so your punk ass is violating the home where my nieces live at. Stay the fuck away from them and if I hear that you are around them I will kill you with my bare fucking hands. Do you fuckin understand me? Punk ass motherfucker, ass can barely piss straight but got the nerves to bring bitches to my niece's house to fuck in her bed." Uncle Bruno slams Nano across the room.

"Yes, sir. Ugh! I am so sorry, Rhema." Nano cried out in pain.

"Shut the fuck up! I am tired of your raggedy ass." I bellowed.

I hated Nano with all of my heart now. After seeing him fucking Jessica in our bed all of the love that I did have left for Nano was gone. Fuck, love!

"Rhema, grab that box with London toys so that we can get the fuck out of here!" Tika bellowed.

"Okay!" I grabbed the box.

"I got that! Just take your little ass to the car." Uncle Bruno ordered me.

"Alright," I obeyed, grabbing my keys from the kitchen counter.

This has been one hell of a day.

Chapter 3
Tika

"I was about to go ham on Nano but Uncle Bruno came through like the soldier that he is," I told Rhema.

"Right, I thought that I was about to die. Nano has never pulled a stunt like that before. Rhema shook her head in amazement that she was still alive.

"Never underestimate anyone especially if they have been acting shady," I advised Rhema.

"Where do you want this box?" Uncle Bruno asked Rhema.

Oh, just put it in the back seat. Thanks, Unk." Rhema opened the door for him.

"No, problem. Promise me one thing." Uncle Bruno glared into my eyes.

"What is it?" Rhema asked him.

"Stay away from that knucklehead, Nano. The word around time is that nigga is that he is on that K2 shit. That shit is bad and I promise you that you don't want any parts of it." Uncle Bruno warned Rhema.

"Woah! I didn't know anything about Nano abusing drugs. Isn't that shit like incense or potpourri or something?" Rhema was stunned.

No wonder Nano and Rhema's relationship was shot to hell. Drugs will kill relationships, vibes, and brain cells. I don't fuck with none of that shit. Rhema is too pretty to be caught up in that scene.

"Everything is starting to make a whole lot of sense now. Nano has been acting out of the norm these last few months." I blurted.

"Right, Tika, but Uncle Bruno, why did you show up when you did? I was not expecting you but I am glad that you did." Rhema hugged her Uncle tightly.

"I was at work when Kossi gave me a call.

My wife told me that she had been trying to reach you but you were not answering. Kossi didn't want to bring London over to your place just in case there was some bullshit going on. I didn't want my wife in the middle of no shit so I volunteered to check up on you." Uncle Bruno explained.

"Thank goodness, she called you when she did or my ass may have been toast." Rhema sighed heavily.

"It's over now. Go home," My Uncle ordered me.

"I am going to drop this stuff off and go get London. Tika and I are taking the kids out to eat but I promise to go straight home afterward." Rhema pleaded with her Uncle.

"Okay, baby! Please leave your location on your phone and turn on the tracking device that I installed on your vehicle." Uncle Bruno advised Rhema.

"I will. I love you, and will see you at home." Rhema happily told him.

"I love you too, baby. You girls, be careful these streets are more dangerous than they look." Uncle Bruno warned Rhema and me before pulling off.

We got into our rides and pulled off. It wasn't long before Rhema was calling me.

"Hello."

"Do you want to grab Alan and then meet me back at Kossi's house? I need to take a hot shower. I got all of this blood and sweat on me from fuckin Jessica up." Rhema asked me.

"I think that I should drop all of your things at Kossi's so that Alan won't feel crowded," I muttered.

I didn't want to ride around the world with all of her shit in my truck. Where the fuck do they do that shit at?

"Okay, I just wanted to see what you wanted to do." Rhema calmly told me.

Chapter 4
Kossi

Bruno just informed me what was going on with Rhema. The story was unbelievable. Nano needed his ass beat and if I had been there his ass would have lost his life. One thing I don't play about is Rhema.
"Kossi, Tika, and I put my things in the garage for now," Rhema claimed.

"Good, baby. Bruno told me about Nano. I am so happy that you are alright." I embraced Rhema tightly.
"Auntie, I love you. Thanks for always being concerned about me." Rhema lovingly spat at me.
"I love you, to the moon and back, sweetie!" I bellowed.
"Where's London?" Rhema asked me.
"She's sleeping." I laughed.

"Auntie, you have the magic touch!" Rhema exclaimed.
"I don't know about all of that!" I laughed. "Since London is sleeping, do you mind if I go out with Tika and her son? I was going to take London with us but I don't want to wake her." Rhema asked me.
"Sure, it's fine. If you wake London she will be very grumpy." I muttered.

*

Rhema took a hot shower before putting on a crop top and jeans. She spun around to look in the mirror that was in the corner of her bedroom. Her phone rang.
"Are you ready?" Tika spat in Rhema's ear.
"Almost, what's up?" Rhema asked Tika.
"I am on my way to get you. There is no reason to take two vehicles." Tika told Rhema.
"You are right! It is a waste of gas. Have you seen the latest gas prices? Ugh!" Rhema sighed heavily.

"I am pumping gas now. Be ready when I pull up!" Tika ended the call.

Rhema quickly pulled her flat iron through her hair and put lip gloss on her lips. She was ready to go so she grabbed her purse and keys.

"Kossi, I will be back later!" She shouted.

"Okay, Rhema, please be safe. Call me if you need me because I am coming like a bat out of hell!" I shouted back.

"Ok, I love you!" Rhema uttered flying out the door.

I got up to lock the door and that's when I saw a black Honda pull up behind Tika. A bunch of bitches got out and raced toward Rhema.

Rhema was still on my property.

"Run up on my baby if you want to. I got something for all five of you bitches!" I hollered.

Tika popped her trunk and pulled out her baseball bat.

"Shut up you old bitch and take your ass into the house!" Jessica screamed at me.
"Jessica, don't disrespect my auntie like that. I will kill all of you wack ass bitches over her so watch your mouth, hoe!" Rhema snarled, taking her gun out of her purse. I ran into the broom closet to get my shotgun but I also sent Bruno a 911 text.
"Kill me! Ha ha, you have got jokes. If anyone is going to die today it's you I didn't come to play with you, girl. You caught me off guard at Nano's house but I'm here to get my lick back," Jessica growled at Rhema.
Jessica and the other ladies proceeded to run up on Rhema and that's when Rhema pulled out her weapon.
"Back up! Don't you see this bitch has a gun?
I am calling the police!"Shirley screamed.

"Don't bother because I am licensed to carry. Which one of you bitches got a death wish tonight? Say the word and I will take you out of your misery for free!" Rhema snarled.

"Hang the damn phone up, Dottie!" Jessica yelled at her sister.

"Why sis?" Dottie wailed.

"Because we are in the wrong because we are on their property!" Jessica explained.

"Fuck, man! Ugh! We will check that bitch later." Dottie grumbled.

I could tell that they were all mad as hell but ask me do I give a fuck?

Tika busted the car windows out! The glass went every which way.

"Bitch, what the fuck are you doing that's my car!" Zaria screamed at Tika.

"Now who coming back fuckin with Rhema later? I thought I heard a bitch say something." Tika bellowed.

"Nah, we're good! By the way, you can have Nano black ass. I don't want him." Jessica scoffed.

"Let me tell your stupid ass one thing! You can not give back what was never yours, trash can Annie!" Rhema retorted.

"So are you saying that I never had him? Didn't you just catch us fuckin in your bed?" Jessica badgered Rhema.

"Only a grimy-ass bitch would ask me that shit after she has gotten her ass beat. To answer your question, yeah I saw you and you looked like a cheap porn star. I don't want Nano ass anymore. What am I going to do with him? You can keep him since he thought that it was okay to fuck up our entire family relationship over some community pussy." Rhema retorted.

"Oh, bitch, you have got me fucked up!" Jessica angrily ran up in Rhema's face.

"Don't come closer back the fuck up now!" Rhema warned Jessica.

Boom. Boom.
The next thing I heard was gunshots.
"This bitch killed my sister! Somebody call 911 and tell them to send an ambulance. OH MY GOD!" Dottie screamed as Jessica fell. There was blood everywhere.
"I am on it, cuzzo!" Brandy screamed.
I had already hit the emergency alarm that I had installed. The police were already on their way.
"Kossi, I didn't mean to kill that bitch!" Rhema wailed.
"Yes, you did, you fuckin bitch!" Zaria fumed at Rhema.
"Shut up, bitch before I murder your dumb ass. I don't know why you bitches are at my Aunt's house pressing me about a nigga that I caught Jessica cheating with. Nano was my man but like I said you can have him. If the dead bitch wants him then she can do whatever she wants. I don't give two shits anymore.

"If Jessica is dead, why would she want Nano? Please make It make sense."

"She's a weird ass bitch!" Samantha chimed in.

"All that I know is you ignorant ghetto ass bitches better stay the fuck from around me before you end up just like Jessica," Rhema warned them all.

"Put the gun down and put your hands up where I can see them." A cop bellowed. Bruno pulled into our driveway. There was a lot of commotion going on.

"What happened to the cop?" The cop pressed Rhema after placing her into handcuffs.

"I was minding my business and about to go out with my friend Tika when all these bitches pulled up behind Tika and jumped out of the car. They were talking all kinds of shit and I feared for my life. The dead girl Jessica rushed up to me and I blasted her ass. The end." Rhema reported to the cop.

My neighbor Marilyn caught everything on camera. She was showing the recording to some of the cops while they placed Rhema inside the cop car.

I was crying. I couldn't believe that these little hoes came here to try to harm Rhema.

"Excuse me, but Rhema is licensed to carry. It was self-defense." I uttered loudly.

The ambulance had arrived at the scene. Jessica was dead as a doorknob. Her goons were steadily popping shit. I had something for their asses though but the cops were there so I just those hoes talk.

"I can't believe that rat ass bitch killed Jessica. I just want to snap Rhema's neck. Ain't no bitch worth me popping my nails off especially not in front of the fuckin police." Dottie snarled looking my way.

I fight young and old bitches so what's up, boo? Don't let this house gown and robe fool your dumb ass. I probably already beat the shit out of your mama's ass back in the day. Little bitch, I promise you that this ain't what you want ever!" I angrily retorted.

"Fuck you!" Dottie hissed at me.

"Wait a minute, now! Don't talk to my wife like that, what's wrong with you?" Bruno defended me.

"You are not my daddy so don't tell me what the fuck to say!" Dottie growled at Bruno and then turned and rolled her eyes at me.

"No, fuck yourself! By the way, just go read a book or something." I howled.

Bruno disliked that this little young and dumb bitch was insulting me the way that she was. It was like the bitch had no respect for anyone especially, not even herself.

"These young women were trespassing, Sir! We do not know any of them. Can you please arrest them for harassment and trespassing?" Bruno pleaded with the cop. If Rhema had to go down to jail then these half-raised ass bitches were going to be right with her.

"Give me a minute, Sir." The cop responded to Bruno.

I glared at the stupid young lady. I felt sorry for her in a way because I could tell that she just wanted to be loved by someone. Dottie seemed so lost. I wondered what her childhood had been like because her attitude was very ridiculous.

"What the fuck are you looking at?" Dottie continued with her foolishness.

"Nothing much." I sighed.

"Leave that woman alone!" Zaria exclaimed to Dottie.

"No, they are the reason that my sister is dead. How will I tell my mother and father about all of this? They will surely kick my ass for allowing her to come to these folks' houses." Dottie whimpered.

"This has gone way too far and for what over a sorry ass nigga that ain't got shit.

"For real Nano, definitely ain't worth dying for or doing 25 to life for." Brandy screeched.

"Brandy, you nailed that shit! Had I known that Jessica's beef was over Nano's sorry ass I wouldn't have ever come here!" Samantha wailed.

"You need to stop talking to that lady like that, Dottie. She's grown and you shouldn't be disrespecting your elders like that. That lady ain't did shit to you!" Brandy raised her voice at Dottie.

"Leave me the fuck alone! I said what I said and I meant what I said!" Dottie bellowed.

Harold and Nina pulled up. They were Dottie's and Jessica's parents.

"What happened to Jessica?" Nina howled when she noticed her dead daughter lying on my property.

"Ma, she had some beef with this bitch daughter." Dottie pointed at me.

"Huh!" Nina looked confused.

Look ma, I know that sometimes you are a little slow but this old bitch daughter killed Jessica over a nigga." Dottie retorted.

"What? Why in the hell are you girls way the fuck over here? Who the hell is Nano?" Nina howled.

"Jessica was messing around with this fine ass nigga named, Nano," Dottie answered her mother.

Nina slapped the hell out of Dottie.

"Why in the fuck are you putting your hands on me?" Dottie screamed.

"You are not only disrespecting yourself but you are disrespecting this lady and me. Why are you using that type of language? You know that we don't allow any of our kids to cuss at us." Nina fumed. Nina seemed very apologetic about her daughter's actions.

"Your mother is right! Jessica is dead and you will be next to her soon if you don't stop all of this ghetto ass nonsense. I can't believe that my daughter just got killed over some dick. I am very disappointed in both of you!" Harold's blood was boiling.

"But, Dad!

"I don't want to hear shit! Close your goddamn mouth." Harold screamed.

We are going to let Rhema go." The cop told us.

"Why? She murdered my daughter!" Nina questioned the cop with a bewildered look on her face.

"All the evidence shows that it was self-defense. All the other young ladies will be arrested and transported to jail." The cop explained.

"Why?

"They were harassing Rhema and trespassing." The cop further explained as he cuffed Dottie.

"I don't want to go to jail. Dad, please help me!" Dottie was frightened.

"There is nothing that I can do to help you. I have pressing matters to take care of like making arrangements for your dead sister. You were a part of this mess and now you have to find a way out of it. I am sorry and I love you." Harold told Dottie.

"Ma, don't let him do this. I thought that I was important to you both." Dottie screamed at the top of her lungs.

"Stop all of that screaming. Dottie, you are embarrassing yourself!" Harold ordered his daughter.

You are sweetie, but you are not a priority at the moment. You are alive and well but your sister isn't. I will see you when you get out." Nina walked away.

"Thank God that someone recorded everything because it could have easily been over for my life," Rhema uttered relieved.

"It sure could have.

"That bird bitch busted out my car windows!" Zaria wailed as she was read her rights.

"You win stupid prizes when you decide to come on someone's property and harass them. I don't want to hear one more word about it unless you want to catch another charge." The officer said with authority.

"Stop being a baby! We can get your windows fixed once we get Terrell to pay our bail." Samantha told her sister Zaria.

"Yeah, but how do I explain this shit to him? You know he just warned me about hanging out with Jessica. He said that she was nothing but trouble and that I should stop being her friend." Zaria whimpered. Zaria knew that Terrell was going to beat her ass about this. They were newlyweds and she should have been home washing clothes and cooking instead of following behind Jessica. Terrell wasn't very abusive but he just sometimes hurt her badly when he became angry.

"Don't worry about it right now because right now we have bigger fish to fry." Samantha retorted.

Once everything was settled I decided to go inside my home for a big glass of wine. My nerves were shot.

"Kossi, Tika, and I are going to head out to eat and chill," Rhema said, clutching her bag.

"Be careful, sweetie." I retorted.

"I will, Auntie," Rhema assured me.

I was worried but just decided to pray.

Chapter 5
Terrell

I was picking up little TJ from Shana's house. I wished the bitch would drop him off at the house but she always had to be difficult all the time. I knew she was trying to get me to come over to her house so that we can fuck. Those days are over since I met Zaria. I wasn't going to mess up my marriage for Shana when I already knew that she wasn't about anything and didn't want to change into a mature woman. I needed more than pussy and head games in my life. It's a shame that I figured out what I wanted after I had gotten Shana pregnant. I love my son and that's the only reason that Shana ever gets to see any part of me is because of TJ.

"Come in for a minute." Shana smiled at me.

I could tell by the way she was smiling that Shana was up to something.

"I don't have time for that. My wife is waiting on me." I rejected Shana.

"Please, I want to show you what I did to TJ's room." Shana pleaded with me.

"Daddy, come see my room!" TJ was now pleading with me.

Fuck!

"Okay, son. You can show me but afterward, we have to go," I muttered.

"Okay, daddy!" TJ pulled me towards his bedroom.

"Wow! It looks great." I glanced around the room.

His mom had redecorated his room with dinosaurs. There were dinosaur stickers on the walls, the bed had the bedding, and the floor had a dinosaur carpet. Our little guy has been very interested in dinosaurs lately so it made a lot of sense

"It's a cool kid room. I love it! Shana, you did a great job!" I congratulated her.

"Thanks," Shana smiled at me.

"You are welcome," I muttered while taking a look inside the closet.

I made a mental note to have my wife purchase TJ a few outfits.

"TJ.Baby, go watch tv for a few minutes while I talk with your daddy." Shana told TJ.

"Okay, momma." TJ obeyed his mother.

Shana tried to push me onto TJ's bed. Hey, what are you trying to do?" I snarled at Shana.

The bitch had caught me off guard with this one. I know it's not right to refer to my son's mother as a bitch but she was so ratchet that I just couldn't help myself.

"Lay down for me. I am trying to see something." Shana giggled.

"See what? There is nothing to see!" I bellowed loudly, pushing Shana away.

"I just want to smell your dick!" Shana said in a seductive voice that didn't turn me on.

"For what it's not yours anymore? I am married, remember! " I growled at her silly ass.

"Oh, I just got caught up looking at all of your huge muscles. I started longing for your big strong arms wrapped around me. Whew! Excuse me! I almost forgot about your petty-ass wife for a moment. Mmm. I need you to get the fuck out of my house so that I can take a shower. I need to call my man to come fuck me all over this house!" Shana snarled, showing me the door.

"Have a nice night! I don't want to keep you from getting fucked!

"Come on TJ let's go! I am sure Zaria is waiting on us at home." I snickered.

My phone's text message notifications kept blowing up. I wondered what the urgency was while I buckled TJ into his car seat. I noticed Shana staring out the front window at me. I stuck my middle finger up at her as I got into my truck. I then looked at my phone and it was Nate telling me that Zaria had gotten arrested for trespassing and that Jessica had gotten murdered. I started beating on the steering wheel because I had just told Zaria about that trouble-making bitch, Jessica.

I decided to take TJ to my mom's house until I figured out if I could get my wife out of jail.

*

"Come on, TJ!" I said, helping him out of the car seat.

"But Daddy, this isn't your house!" TJ exclaimed.

"I know! Dad has to run a few errands and I am going to need you to stay with Grandma Geneva until I get back." I told my son.

"Son, what are you doing here?" Geneva happily questioned me.

"Zaria is locked up. Can you keep an eye on TJ for me?" I pleaded.

"Of course. I would love that. Go on now and hurry on to see about your wife. Zaria doesn't belong in nobody's jail." Geneva's face beamed with joy.

"Thanks, mom, I'll be back as soon as I can." I hurried out of the house.

I jumped into my ride and headed straight for the police station. I had a couple of thousand dollars on me plus my Mastercard. I hoped that her bail wouldn't be too much.

I finally got to the police station. There was a line so I had to wait my turn.

"Can I help you?" A woman asked me with a notepad in her hand.

"I am here to post bail for my wife," I explained to the lady.

"What's your wife's full name?" She asked.

"Zaria Stevenson," I answered her. "You can have a seat and I will be right back in a few minutes." The woman pointed to a waiting area.

"Thanks," I uttered.

My phone rang. I didn't recognize the number but I quickly answered it in case it was my wife.

"Hello!"

"Terrell! I am in jail. Can you please come get me." Zaria pleaded with me.

"I am already here, baby! Just hold on tight." I told my wife.

"Can you get Samantha out of here because she's with me?" Zaria whimpered.

"Yes, I got you and your sister. Stop crying, you will both be out soon!" I bellowed.

"I can't help it! Jessica was killed in front of me. I will never forget the sound of the gunshots." Zaria's voice sounded shaky.

"Baby, I warned you about Jessica. I know

that she is your friend but she was a skanky hoe." I grunted.

I didn't like to speak ill of the dead but Jessica wasn't a Saint.

"I know and I am so sorry! I should have listened to you. I never imagined that someone would die especially not over some nigga that was for everybody." Zaria wailed.

"Jessica got murdered over a nigga?" I raised my voice.

"Bae, she was messing with Nano. His lady caught them in the bed fuckin. Jessica got beat up by the lady. Jessica was all in her feelings and wanted revenge so we all went to the lady's, mama's house and all the shit went down." Zaria wiped her tears on her sleeve.

"Damn, that's a shame because Nano will not grieve over that bitch. I know that nigga very well. He's friends with one of my brothers." I shook my head.

"Sir, can you step this way?" The woman with the notepad asked me.

"Sure. One moment, please. I am on a call.

I have to go now, I love you." I concluded the call.

"Your wife's bail is $100." She told me.

"I would like to post bail for Samantha Griffin," I uttered, pulling out my Mastercard.

"Of course let me pull her name up. Samantha's bail will be $50." She announced.

I quickly swiped my card and waited for my wife and her sister so that we could get the hell away from this place.

About twenty minutes went by before Zaria and Samantha were released. I spun my wife around and kissed her passionately.

"Bae, put me down I feel dirty and icky from this nasty ass jail." Zaria frowned.

"I don't give a damn if you smelled like a skunk. I will burn this bitch down to get to you, baby." I retorted.

"Awe, they say true love is hard to find." Samantha giggled.

"Someone lied. I found my soulmate and only true love on a cloudy day at the park." Zaria squealed.

"I need to pick up TJ from mom's house," I told my wife.

"I forgot that it was our weekend to get him. I am sorry about all of this mess, babe." Zaria muttered.

"I know that you are. Just listen to me when I tell you something because all of this shit could have been avoided." I grunted.

"I certainly will because jail is not for me. It's so damn nasty in there. I can't fathom why people visit there so frequently." Zaria sounded very disgusted.

"Neither can I." Samantha shook her head.

Chapter 6
Harold

I couldn't believe that we are now planning my daughter's funeral. I always dreamed of walking Jessica down the aisle so that she could marry her King. My heart was broken.

"I can't believe that girl got away with killing my baby." Nina wept uncontrollably.

"The law is the law. Jessica was in the wrong but she didn't have to take her life." I shrugged my shoulders.

It was taking everything in me to be strong for my wife but had suffered a great loss as well. I wanted to hit something or somebody. I had to be strong for my wife. I could break down privately when she was busy running some errands or something.

"Fuck the goddamn law! I want that heffa dead. If Jessica can't live her life why should she? I say an eye for an eye. A life for a life." Nina screamed, picking up her favorite vase and throwing it across the room.

"That's enough, honey! I think that it's time that you take a nice relaxing bath." I said lovingly.

"I don't want to take a freakin bath! I want Jessica back here with us.

"We can't! God needed her more than we did. I am sorry." I babbled.

There was banging at the door.

"I'll get it!" Nina groaned.

It was Tabby.

"You look like a hot ass mess!" Nina's sister muttered upon entering my home.

"I know. I know. I just can't get my shit together since reality has set in about Jessica." Nina wept.

"I understand, hun. I just couldn't get anyone to cover my shift or I would have been here sooner." Tabby explained to Nina.

"Good evening, Tabby!" I bellowed.

"Hi, there, brother n law. I am so sorry about what happened to Jessica." Tabby responded sadly to me.

"Me too, it was sudden and very unexpected. I keep pinching myself because I am hoping that this is just a dream. I want to wake up and things will be back to normal." I sighed heavily.

"Wouldn't that be wonderful?" Tabby shook her head.

"Tabby, can you help Nina with her shower? I think that she needs some rest." I suggested.

"Of course, come on sister, let's go get you cleaned up." Tabby agreed with me.

I don't wanna move. I am just overcome with grief." Nina complains.

"I have a little remedy that will get you moving. There is nothing that a little prayer can't boost." Tabby had some much compassion for her sister.

I watched as Tabby held my wife's hands and prayed for her strength in the Lord. Her words eased my mind and A few minutes after the prayer Nina was goofing off like she always did when her sister came around. They were now upstairs preparing for the shower.

People were texting and calling me. They were asking me what we needed. I told my brother Kason to bail Dottie out of jail for me. Everyone else I told to do what they think was right and that they could come over tomorrow after 12. I didn't want to be bothered by loud company. It was not a time for celebration for me. My daughter was deceased and I was still trying to wrap my head around that.

My guilty pleasure was drinking but I was trying to quit because it wasn't good for my health. I decided to have a drink because I needed something to help me cope with all that was going on.

Chapter 7
Nina

I knew that Tabby and Harold were only trying to help but a sister was hurt by this great tragedy. Things will never be the same around here without Jessica. She was the life source of this house. My daughter was such a happy person. She would dance and sing all day long. Jessica always gave a helping hand whenever she could.
"Sis, I can't believe that Jess is gone. I just kept praying that she would walk through the door." I whimpered.
"I can't either. It seemed like yesterday when you were pregnant with her. You were so happy about having a baby girl." Tabby relayed.
"Yes, I was but I have a confession to make," I whispered.
"What is it?" Tabby asked with curiosity.

"Jessica is not Terrell's daughter." I quickly spat.

"What are you talking about, sis?" Tabby exclaimed.

"I had a one-night stand with Jessie Brown." I breathed.

"What? When did this happen?" Tabby blurted.

"Long ago in my wild and crazy times. I had a little too much to drink. I told Jessie about my pregnancy and we agreed to keep our love child a secret." I revealed getting up to close and lock my bedroom door.

"Why? What you are saying doesn't make any sense to me. Jessie is a very wealthy man. He could have easily taken care of his daughter!' Tabby bellowed.

"Didn't you know that he was married to that wealthy half-breed woman? Her white daddy would have had Jessie skinned for stepping out on her. So we kept silent all of these years. A decision had to be made and so here we are. Jessie was not a deadbeat dad." I whispered, squeezing my hands.

"I never saw Jessie Brown around here taking care of that girl!" Tabby stammered.

"But I did. For instance, he bought this house and the three cars that Dottie, Jessica, and I drive. I never paid for anything when it came to my daughters. Dottie is not his child, she belongs to Harold. We needed it to look like Jessica wasn't being favored over Dottie. Jessie paid for their private schooling, college, vacations, grooming, etc." I explained.

"So Harold never knew," Tabby asked.

"Never but I must confess the truth to him tonight because Jessie Brown is going to want to be involved in his daughter's arrangements." I wept.

"How are you going to tell Harold something like that at a time like this? The man's heart is already broken. If you make this known to him now you will surely hurt his pride." Tabby warned me.

"It's out of my hands," I replied weakly.

"When are you going to tell Jessie Brown?" Tabby questioned me.

"I emailed him the news so I expect to hear from him soon. I am sure that he will make the arrangements. Jessie may not be in Jessica's life physically but he loved her with his heart and soul. When she was a baby he would come to sit with her for hours. We would meet up at a secret location but those visits stopped when she was about 8 years old. We didn't want Jessica to accidentally tell Harold about our secret meetings. Jessie showered his daughter with loads of love, gifts, and attention. He was very crazy about her." I spat.

Chapter 8
Rhema

Alan, Tika, and I were seated by a window seat at the seafood restaurant. I strapped Alan into a highchair while Tika went outside to take a call from her boo, Drake.
"Auntie, where is London? I want to play with London!" Alan whines.
I hoped that Alan wasn't about to show his ass up in this restaurant. I wasn't in the mood to be trying to calm him down. If he shows out on me I am taking his little behind to his mother.
"Maybe, tomorrow. London couldn't come with us because she fell asleep." I explained to Alan.
"I am sleepy too," Alan admitted, yawning. After dinner, your mommy will take you home and get you ready for bed." I told Alan.
He was very talkative for his age.

"I am so sorry about that. Drake is such a needy asshole." Tika giggled.

"Don't do that!" I scolded Tika.

"What?" She glared at me.

"You love that nigga's dirty draws so don't be calling him an asshole. He loves you and is faithful to you, unlike Nano." I retorted.

"You are so right! I need to cut that out. I am blessed and most women don't get that lucky." Tika sighed.

"I am most women." I sulked.

"I am not talking about you, Rhema. There is someone out here for you, girlfriend. Please don't call it quits yet. Nano is not the cream of the crop with his community dick having ass." Tika assured me.

"Yes, maybe you are right." I agreed so I decided to adjust my attitude.

I am young and beautiful so any man would love to have me on their team. I cooked, cleaned and I knew how to suck dick. I was a good candidate to become not only someone's girlfriend but I would make a great wife to the right man.

We ordered food but I couldn't eat so I had the waitress bring me a takeout container. Tika was chomping away but I couldn't eat because Jessica was so heavy on my mind. Seeing her body crashing to the ground after those bullets riddled her body kept replaying in my mind while my eyes were opened.

"What's wrong with you?" Tika eyed me suspiciously.

"I just can't get Jessica off my mind," I grunted.

"You need to chill because that bitch got what she deserved. Rhema, you defended yourself and that's what any law-abiding citizen would have done." Tika reminded me.

"It may be true and all but I am not a killer so the shit is bothering me. I hadn't planned on killing anyone when I woke up this morning." I complained.

"True, but Jessica was so pressed by that ass whipping that you had given her that she couldn't let it go. Don't blame yourself because it was not your fault. We all make our own choices. Jessica chose to fuck YOUR man in Your bed. What the fuck did she think was going to happen? Had it been me I probably would have killed her ass in the house. Then she had the nerve to come to Kossi's with a bunch of bitches like she's about that life. Have you asked yourself how she knew where Kossi lived? I am telling you that the bitch was pressed for real because why play detective and bring that shit to Kossi's like that? I am trying to tell you that there is more to this than meets the eye. The bitch could have been planning to kill you for all that we know. Look at the great lengths that she took to get to you. They say if you live by the sword you will die by the sword." Tabby bellowed.

"What you are saying is true. I never looked at it that way. I guess we will never know how she found out where I was at. Maybe Nano told her." I thought.

"Maybe, but fuck that nigga, unless you just want him back," Tika smirked.

"Hell no! He ain't for me." I grumbled.

I was mad that Tika would think that I would want to take Nano back. I would be foolish to take him back after all I went through today.

"Good because you deserve better and there is someone out there waiting to meet you." Tika smiled at me.

"I believe that!" I giggled.

After dinner, Tika took me home. Bruno, Kossi, and London were all sleeping. It had been a long day and tomorrow would probably be longer since I would be job hunting. I decided to go right to bed.

Chapter 9
Nano

My sister Kinena came over to clean up my spot since Jessica and Rhema had destroyed it fighting over me. "This doesn't make any damn sense, Nano! You know that you were raised better than this. Why would you bring some slut over here to fuck in the bed that you share with Rhema? Haven't your dumbass ever heard of a damn hotel? Geesh, how dumb can you get?" Kinena scolded me as she cleaned the apartment.

"Sis, I don't have any money for a hotel. I always brought girls home while Rhema was out. I never got caught before." I admitted.

"Well, there is a first time for everything and look at how your the relationship has been destroyed. I thought that you loved Rhema?" Kinena badgered me.

"I do love her but I love having sex with other women," I confessed.

What kind of love is that? I am sure that Rhema would have a word or two to say to you about this." Kinena shook her head.

"Rhema is gone for good! Her uncle threatened to kill me if I bothered her again." I sighed heavily.

"What about London?" Kinena muttered.

"I love my daughter but I am not in any position right now to be caring for her. I have to work to pay these fuckin bills." I grunted.

"That's the problem, you need a regular paying job. Can't you see that these streets don't love anybody? How long do you plan on slinging dope? London needs her dad around to teach her and guide her throughout life. You can't do that if you are dead or locked up." Kinena preached to me.

"I know. I am thinking about going back to school. I am three months short of completing my business degree." I bellowed.

"It's about time!" Kinena yelped.

"Nano!" Vashawn screamed running into the apartment.

"Why are you screaming? You just scared the hell out of me!" Kinena jumped.

"Jessica is dead!" Vashawn announced.

"What? I don't understand!" I yelled.

"Rhema shot Jessica to death," Vashawn explained to us.

I couldn't believe what I was hearing. I knew that Jessica was a hot head but for her to keep fuckin with Rhema after she had gotten her ass whipped was crazy.

"Who's Jessica?" Kinena asked, bewildered.

"The girl that Rhema caught me with earlier. This is all my fault. Shit!" I exclaimed.

"Nano, now you see why you need to be just a one-woman man!" Kinena argued.

"Sis, leave me alone!" I snarled.

"Okay, but where is my weed at? I am ready to go home to my man and children.

"What weed?" I questioned my sister.

"The weed that you are going to give me for cleaning up your shitty apartment! I didn't come here to do this for free." Kinena glared at me like she was ready to put her foot in my ass.

"Okay, damn, sis. I got you." I told her.

"Thank you. I love you and I will see you soon." Kinena accepted the weed and was on her way.

I sat at the kitchen table.

"Are you okay?" Vashawn asked me. No! I was about to call Jessica and have her spend the night with me. I can't believe that she is no longer with us." I held my head in my hands.

I felt defeated.

"I am sorry. I didn't want to be the bearer of bad news." Vashawn stuttered.

"It's okay, eventually I would have found out. Thanks for coming by." I slapped him up.

"You are welcome. You are my dawg, I am always going to look out no matter what. I am so sorry for your loss." Vashawn muttered.

"Jessica was a good person and I liked her. It was not just

sex for me. I was feeling her whole vibe." I shook my head.

"I understand. Your baby mama has to be crazy as hell to just kill someone like that." Vashawn retorted.

"Rhema is crazy but she has a conscience. I am sure it's eating her up. I wonder what happened because Rhema would never have pulled out her weapon unless she felt threatened. She can fight her ass off." I told Vashawn.

"I wasn't there so I honestly don't have a clue. Why don't you call Rhema and ask her what happened?" Vashawn replied.

"It wouldn't be wise of me to do that. Her Uncle told me to stay away from heroes. I will have to wait until shit simmers down before I reach out to Rhema." I clasped my hands together.

I am out of suggestions." he uttered.

Chapter 10
Jessie

Every night before I turn in I checked my emails to see if Nina needed anything for herself or my daughter. Tonight was no different from any other night. I opened Nina's email and gasped at the words that I read. My namesake was murdered tonight. Tears spilled from my eyes as memories of days long past flashed before me. I remember holding my precious daughter as a baby and chasing her around the yard as a toddler. All the gifts that I hand-picked especially for her. My sweet Jessica was now resting in peace with the Lord.

I called Keith my driver and told him to meet me at the front gate in twenty minutes. I needed to handle some things concerning my child.

I went into my bedroom where my wife Donna was crocheting. I picked out a sweatsuit and put it on.
"Where are you going at this hour of the night?" My wife asked me.
"I have some pressing business that needs to be handled immediately," I explained, trying to fight my tears.
"What type of business?" Donna pressed me.
"Nothing that concerns you, honey," I said politely.
"Jessie, don't push me away! I want to help if I can." Donna bellowed.
"Donna, don't be angry with me!" I wailed.
"Why would I be angry with you? Jessie, did you do something bad? Do you need counsel?" Donna badgered me relentlessly with her questions.
"After we married I found out that this girl that I had sex with was

pregnant. I kept the child a secret for all of these years because I was afraid that your father would destroy my life." I confessed.

"My God! Jessie, I am so sorry that you had to do that. My father was very old-fashioned. Has something happened to your child?" Donna questioned me.

"She was murdered. I need to make the funeral arrangements." I sniffled.

"Honey, allow me to accompany you. I promise you that I am not angry. I just want to support you. I would want the same thing from you if Donnia Regina wasn't yours." Donna embraced me.

"Very well. Let's go." I sighed heavily. What's her name?

"What did you say, dear?" I looked up at Donna.

"What's your daughter's name? Jessica." I stammered.

"Jessie, I hope that you gave her the best life possible." Donna looked me into my eyes.

"Yes, I did! Everything that I ever gave to Donnia Regina I gave to Jessica Regine." I retorted.

"Regine, huh? Did you pick out her middle name?" Donna asked me.

"Yes, she couldn't have my last name so I gave her part of my first name and middle name," I explained.

"Jessie, you are a good man. I love you, thanks for trusting me with your secret after all of these years." Donna smiled at me.

"It is good to get it off my chest. Keeping this secret from you bothered me more than you would ever know. I just couldn't risk your father finding out." I told her.

"It's alright. I would have done the same thing. My daddy wasn't understanding anything. He was always trying to tell us how to run our marriage." Donna relayed.

*

My wife went to the funeral home to make Jessica's final arrangements. We chose the best of everything. I want my daughter's service to be fit for royalty.

Afterward, we decided to visit Nina. I didn't know if her husband knew anything about me but he was about to find out who was footing the bills all these years.

A man answered the door. I assumed he was Harold, Nina's husband.

"Is Nina around? I came to pay my condolences." I politely muttered.

"Yes, she's upstairs resting but you are welcome to come inside. I will go get her." Harold stated.

"Thank you. I am Jessie and this is my wife Donna." I introduced myself to Harold.

Harold paused for a moment before introducing himself. We took a seat in the formal living room.

"This is a beautiful home. Nina has great taste." Donna observed.

"Darling, this is the home that I purchased for them. I wanted my daughter to grow up in a nice neighborhood and have a nice home." I told Donna.

"From what I see you did good by Nina and Jessica. You are a good man Jessie." Donna squeezed my hand.

*

"Nina, you have visitors," I told my wife.

"I am not ready to see anyone!" Nina protested.

"I can't turn the man and his wife away. It would be very rude!" I objected.

"Who are they?" Tabby piped.

"Jessie and Donna," I replied.

Tabby glared at Nina.
"What's going on?" I demanded.
There was silence for a long minute.
"Just go downstairs and wait for me. I will tell you everything that you need to know then." Nina muttered.
I did as my wife asked but I had a weird feeling in the pit of my stomach. My intuition told me that I wouldn't like what was coming.
Dottie entered the house. She slammed the door behind her.
"Daddy, how could you just leave me down there in that filthy jail like that?" Dottie howled, not noticing that we had visitors.
"Dottie, we have visitors right now. We will discuss this later." I told my daughter.
"Whatever, dad!" Dottie replied bitterly running up the stairs to her bedroom.

I felt bad for Dottie but I would have to deal with her later.

Finally, Nina and Tabby joined Jessie, Donna, and me.

Jessica stood up and embraced Nina. The way he held her in his arms made me feel very uncomfortable.

"I am so sorry about Jessica!" Jessie wailed.

"Me too! I can't imagine life without her." Nina bellowed.

I made all of the arrangements for her Homegoing service. Everything has been paid in full. All that is needed now is for you to provide the funeral home with a date for Jessica's services. I will present you the check from the life insurance company when it comes. I do not need it." Jessie declared.

"Can somebody tell me what the hell is going on? Why is this man doing so much for our daughter, Nina!" I growled from frustration.

"He's Jessica's biological father!" Nina informed me.

"What do you mean? I thought I was Jessica's father." I shook my head in disgust.

I had given up a lot when I decided to marry Nina when she had become pregnant with Jessica. I wanted to do the right thing by Nina so I sacrificed the things that I wanted for my little family.

"You heard what I said and it's the truth. Harold, please don't make this harder for me than it already is." Nina said through her hot burning tears while Tabby rubbed her shoulders.

"So you named her after this man! Why didn't you tell me?" I demanded.

"I don't know! I take that back because I didn't want Jessie to lose everything that he worked hard for because of our child. I knew that you would do the honorable thing and accept me and Jessica. Please forgive me." Nina pleaded with me.

"Nina is telling the truth. Had my father found out about Jessie he would have destroyed my husband. My father was a mean racist white man and I had gone against the grain by marrying Jessie, a full-blooded black man. My mother passed for white but my father never knew that she wasn't black. If he had known he probably would have had her murdered. I just found out about Jessica tonight. I don't have an issue with any of this because we weren't married when Jessica was conceived." Donna spoke up for Nina and Jessie.

I just couldn't believe what I was hearing.

"I am sorry, Harold but I tried to make up for all of this by purchasing this home and making sure that the bills that you and Nina accumulated were taken care of. I made sure that the girls had the best of everything, which included their schooling." Jessie brought it to my attention.

"I was wondering how we were able to make it, especially after I got hurt on my job. Nina just told me that she was taking care of it all so I trusted her and didn't worry. Wow!" I uttered in amazement.

I didn't know whether to be happy or angry with Jessie and my wife. Technically we were not married when all of this came about. It was the principle though.

"Just let bygones be bygones. Jessica is no longer with us and she wouldn't want us bickering. She lived a good wholesome life with people who truly loved her." Tabby suggested.

Chapter 11
Rhema

It was now the next morning. I had fallen asleep on the sofa. I went to the bathroom to shower and brush my teeth. Afterward, I fixed my hair and dressed. I had a lot to do today.

"Mommy!" London squealed when she saw me.

"Good morning, sunshine!" I quickly hugged my baby.

"You look good!" Kossi greeted me with a warm smile.

"Thanks, Auntie, and good morning!" I bellowed.

"So where are you off to this morning?" She asked me while pouring some coffee into her cup.

I am not sure yet. The temp agencies seem promising. Maybe, I will start there." I answered my Aunt.

"Sounds like a good plan. Good luck!" Kossi muttered, picking up London and placing her into her high chair.

"I am going to head out!" I kissed London on her forehead.

"You don't want to eat breakfast with us?" Kossi asked me.

"No, ma'am. I will eat this apple and stop at a Coffee shop for a doughnut or something later." I uttered, grabbing an apple from the fruit bowl.

"Be safe!" Kossi bellowed.

*

I was sitting at a table at the temp agency filling out an application when I heard a commotion. I looked up and saw Brandy and Camille, some old friends of mine coming in. They were laughing and carrying on. I ignored them and continued with my paperwork.

"Rhema is that you, girlie!" Brandy exclaimed.

"Hello," I smiled at Brandy and Camille.

"What are you doing here?" Camille questioned me.

"I am applying for a job," I replied.

"Why? I thought that you and Nano were on some Bey and Jay-Z shit!" Camille looked at me strangely.

"Oh, don't believe everything that you hear. Nano has money but not long money and besides, we are no longer together." I retorted.

"Since when?" Camille snorted.

"Yesterday, and I am good on his ass. His love ain't for me! Now if you excuse me, I need to get back to this paperwork because I need a job so that I can provide for my daughter." I smiled.

"I thought that you did hair, nails, lashes, and shit like that." Camile continued to badger me with her questions.

"I do but I don't have any real clientele. I lost most of them when I was pregnant with London." I sadly admitted.

I had so much going for myself before I met Nano. I had to get back to my old self again.

"Give me your number and I will spread the word and you will be popping in no time. I will be your first customer. What you need to be focusing on is getting a shop." Camille advised.

"Thanks." I happily spat.

"Can you do my shit now? I have to be at the strip club by 10 tonight." Camille asked me.

"Sure, I didn't know that you were a stripper," I replied.

"Yes, I have been stripping for two years now. I can send more girls your way if you have the time today." Camille grinned at me.

I need to get some supplies first though. Can you meet me in about half an hour? I will text you the address." I asked.

"I definitely can and I will bring my friends with me," Camille told me.

"Okay, I will see you guys later," I told them, shooting the application into the trash can.

*

"Kossi, can I use the basement as my shop until I can get my own again," I asked my Auntie.

I knew that she would say yes.

"Of course, I thought that you would never ask. I wanted it to be your own decision." Kossi told me.

"Thanks, Auntie, I have another favor to ask. It's kind of huge." I uttered.

"What is it?" Kossi asked me cautiously.

"Can I borrow $1000.00 for supplies?" I pleaded.

"Yes, you can but I am going to give you $2000.00. Things have gone up drastically." Kossi muttered, handing me her Visa card.

"Thanks, Kossi, you won't regret this!" I excitedly hugged her.

"You are welcome." Kossi hugged me back.

"I have to go. My clients will be arriving shortly!" I exclaimed, rushing out of the house.

I loved the way that Kossi supported me. She and Bruno always have my back no matter what. Any moment that I thought I would fail they were always there to encourage and guide me throughout all of my ups and downs. I am glad that they chose to raise me as their own. I owe them so much and I am very thankful.

I couldn't believe that things were going so well for me. I will be earning my own money soon and that was a deal breaker for me.

Chapter 12
Camille

I couldn't wait to get my nappyhead done. I had been meaning to do it myself but something was always coming up. I just threw on my trusty ole blonde wig to save the night when I had to get on the pole. The men were not thinking about my hair; their only concern was being able to see my big tits and phat ass. It was always a competition with these bitches at the strip club so I liked to look my very best at all times.

Brandy and I were now leaving the beauty supply store. I purchased some red 30-inch bundles. I had a fire-ass outfit for tonight to go with it.

Rhema had a nice little shop in her auntie's basement. It was clean and free from dust. Rhema and her auntie was setting up the supplies when we arrived.

"Rhema, go ahead and get started. I will organize everything and then label them after I am done." Kossi told Rhema.

"Auntie, are you sure? I can do it?" Rhema muttered.

"Yes, it's okay. London is sleeping so I have nothing else to do at the moment." Kossi insisted.

"I love your relationship. I wish my auntie was as cool as Kossi!" I shook my head.

"Thanks. Camille." Kossi smiled at me.

I sat in the salon chair while Camille worked her magic on my head. When she washed my hair I thought I was in heaven because of the way that she massaged my scalp.

"Most beauticians don't bother by washing their client's hair. They want you to come washed, blow-dried, and braided down before you come." Brandy revealed.

"I don't like that because they charge an arm and a leg for services that should include all of that with the price they're charging," I complained.

"I always wash my client's hair because I work better with clean hair. I don't go off on someone saying that they just washed their hair." Rhema responded.

"As you should!" Kossi agreed.

"Step over here, please. It's time for you to sit under the dryer." Rhema told me.

It was now Brandy's turn to get her hair washed. The doorbell rang.

"I wonder who that is?" Kossi ran upstairs.

"Hi, I am Karen and this is Paula. We have a lash appointment with Rhema?" Karen sweetly told Kossi.

"Right this way, ladies." Kossi showed them downstairs where they were seated.

"Hello, welcome to my shop!" Rhema greeted the ladies.

"We are here for lashes," Paula explained to Rhema.

"Give me about fifteen minutes and I will be right with you ladies," Rhema told them.

"Cool," Paula mumbled.

An hour later Paula and Karen were on their way out and Rhema was working on my head again. She braided me down and began to sew the bundles into my head.

"Ohh, that's tight!" I cried out.

"Sorry, Camille!" Rhema apologized.

"No pain no gain!" Brandy spat at me.

"So true. Pain is a part of beauty. I can't wait to get my ass on that pole tonight!" I excitedly exclaimed.

"You are going to be popping in all that red hair. All heads are going to be turning in your direction. bestie!" Brandy assured me.

"Thanks." I giggled.

Two hours later Rhema was finished with my hair. I glanced in the mirror. I was amazed at how good my hair looked. Rhema had slayed this hair of mine.

"Thanks, boo! I love it." I said with glee, handing $150 to Rhema.

"You are welcome." Rhema quickly accepted the cash.

Three hours later Brandy was looking like a new woman with her 22-inch water wave bundles in her hair.

"Damn, you look good as fuck." I snapped at Brandy.

"Are you mad or nah?" Brandy asked me.

"I am not mad at all. You look so beautiful." I exclaimed.

Chapter 13
Nina
A few days later

Today was sadly the day that we would lay my eldest daughter to rest. Harold has been keeping to himself a lot after learning that he wasn't Jessica's biological father. I am sorry that I hurt him. It wasn't my intention at all.

I sat at my vanity table and applied my makeup. A tear dropped from my eye as I thought about Jessica.

I didn't know how to feel. I was numb inside. Tabby brushed my hair into a bun before placing my veil on.

"There you go, sis!" Tabby kissed my forehead.

"Thanks for everything, sis." I softly murmured.

"There is no need to thank me. I am just doing my sisterly duties. You are important to me, Nina." Tabby sighed.

"Ditto." I nodded my head.

"Mom, are you almost done? Dad says that the limo will be here in about ten minutes," Dottie notified me.

"Yes, dear. I will be right down." I smiled warmly at Dottie.

"Mom," Dottie called out to me.

"Yes, sweetie," I replied.

"Thanks, for all that you have done for me. I appreciate you!" Dottie whimpered.

"Sweetheart, please don't cry. I will climb mountains and swim the seas for you. Never doubt that." I held Dottie in my arms.

"Enough! We need to be on our way to the church. Save your tears for the funeral." Tabby scolded us both.

"I am sorry, I am just overwhelmed with grief. Learning to live without

Jessica has been very difficult for me. We did everything together. She knows all of my deepest darkest secrets." Dottie sniffled.

"Your mother and I are that way. I am so glad that you had a chance to experience true sisterhood and friendship." Tabby hugged Dottie.

"Me too. Let's go say goodbye." Dottie dabbed her eyes with a tissue.

The ride to the church was dreadfully silent. I don't know what everyone was thinking but my mind was all over the place.

The church was filled with family and friends. I walked up to my daughter's casket. Jessica looked like she was in a deep sleep.

"She looks beautiful," Dottie exclaimed, admiring Jessica's outfit.

"Simply beautiful," I agreed, staring at my lifeless daughter.

I couldn't believe that this was it.

I touched Jessica's face. She was so cold. I wanted to hold Jessica in my arms and warm her up as I did when she was a child.

"Goodbye, my love until we meet again. Please watch over our family. I love you so much." I whispered to Jessica before kissing her on her cheek.

I took a seat next to my parents and Tabby. I watched Harold walk up to Jessica's casket. He started sobbing uncontrollably so I rushed to his side.

"Baby, it's going to be okay." I rubbed his back.

"I miss her so much. I know that she's not mine but I loved her like she was. I am sorry for pushing you away after learning the truth about Jessica's paternity. I want to thank you for choosing me to go through parenthood with you. We had a great life together. We never lacked anything and I am grateful because had it been any other way we would have struggled." Harold spat.

"Oh, honey! I love you so much. We will get through this together." I happily wept.

We walked together hand in hand to our seats in the pew. We watched Jessie, Donna, and Donnia Regina walk up to the casket.

"My baby! Why, my daughter? Why? I want her back with me. There was so much that I wanted to do for her. I wanted to show her the world. Jesus, why did you take her from me so soon?" Jessie howled loudly.

He was in great pain over Jessica's death. Donna and Donnia Regina consoled him. It broke my heart to see Jessie in so much pain. He had done all that he could to make sure that Jessica had the best of everything in life and death.

Chapter 14
3 Months Later
Rhema

Things were going very well for me. The business was booming. Every day was different. Some days I did nails all day or lashes but for the most part, people wanted their hair slayed. My clientele has grown so much. In my free time, I searched for a building to purchase for my shop.

One day when I was out and about I ran into a handsome guy named Judah. He was smart and had his own money. One thing that I refused to do was fuck with a broke man or another drug dealer. Those types of men were not for me. I needed my man or whoever was interested in me to be on my level. I was no longer settling just to have a dick to ride on.

Judah was everything that Nano wasn't and more. To me, he seemed God-sent. He called just to say hello. Judah would surprise me with flowers or dinner but what captured my heart was how he always would include London. If he brought me flowers Judah would bring London a toy. If he brought me lunch Judah would bring London a Happy Meal. I liked that because London and I came as a package. If a man couldn't show love for my daughter then we had no future.

"Rhema, do you want to go to a movie tonight?" Judah asked me. "Sure but it depends on when I am finished with my last client. How about we get a burger and some fries if it's too late for a movie? I am sure that I will be hungry and then we can go for a walk." I suggested.

I knew that I would be tired but I loved spending time with Judah.

"It's a date then. I have to get back to work. I will text you later." Judah told me.

*

I was on my way to the beauty supply store to buy some items when a bitch called my phone.

"Is this Rhema?" A female asked me.

"Yes, may I help you?" I politely asked the caller.

I thought that she was a potential customer.

"Bitch, I don't like you!" The female screamed into my ear.

"Excuse me! Who is this?" I bellowed, the caller had caught me off guard.

I had no idea what she meant.

"I am your worse fuckin nightmare. If you don't let Nano see his daughter I am going to fuck you up!" The caller threatened.

"Haha! Ha! Bitch, you are funny. Do me a favor and use those two lips that you are using to yap on my line and wrap them around my baby dad's dick for me. I think that you'd be better off because bitch, you don't know me because if you did you would use your time on something useful. I don't take threats lightly. Ask the hood about me, boo boo!" I raised my voice.

"I am not worried!" She howled before I clicked her ass off.

I didn't want to hear that shit. I had better things to do. Money was my motivation and not what Nano is doing or wanting. He's an ex for a reason. If this bitch wants to fight then she will have to catch up with me when she can because I stay ready.

One thing that I won't do is argue about a nigga. It's not my style. Fuck Nano and that bitch!

I made my purchases and made my way back to the house.

"Rhema, Nano stopped by here while you were out," Kossi informed me.

"Really, what did he want?" I asked Kossi.

"He wanted to see London," Kossi stated.

"Don't let him see her! Some ghetto ass bitch called me making threats while I was out." I bellowed.

"Threats?" Kossi asked, alarmed.

"She said that I better allow Nano to visit London or she would be my worst nightmare." I relayed.

"What on Earth is going on?" Kossi glared at me.

"I have no idea. I am not thinking about Nano or his goons. He has been pillow-talking to somebody." I grunted.

"She must don't know what happened to the last bitch that approached you about Nano." Kossi shook her head in disbelief.

"Auntie, I don't want to think about it. This is exactly why we are not together and I am so glad that I left him alone. My life has been good ever since." I told Auntie.

"Nobody is going to do shit! I am hiring a security guard, one for the house and one to follow you around when you leave the house." Kossi said with a made-up mind.

"Auntie, what about my privacy?" I complained.

"Your safety is more important. I can't lose you, baby girl." Kossi declared.

"Damn. if it ain't one thing it's another." I said annoyed.

I knew that Kossi had my best interest at heart so I didn't bother about arguing. I knew that I would never win.

The doorbell rang. My client was here and it was time to get to work.

Chapter 15
Dottie

Now that my sister was gone forever I poured myself into my schooling. I am working towards getting my Doctorate in Business. Jessica would party and study together. I wasn't really into partying and the drug scene the way my sister was. I just went along with Jessica because she was my sister. She had met Nano at one of the parties that we had attended. The two had hit it off the first night. They fucked outside in the bushes. I knew that he wasn't shit but Jessica wouldn't listen. I blame Nano for my sister's death because he didn't have to fuck my sister in the house he shared with Rhema. Nano wasn't broke; he could afford a hotel but he wouldn't splurge on Jessica.

"Dottie, I brought you some soup." My cousin Mandy startled me.

"Thanks, I didn't realize how hungry I am." I accepted the bowl of soup.

"You are welcome." Mandy sat on the floor.

"What's on your mind?' I asked Mandy.

"A lot but don't worry about me." Mandy sighed heavily.

"Stop that! I am here for you." I told her.

"Eat your soup and then let's go for a drive. I don't want anyone to overhear what I have to tell you." Mandy grunted.

"Okay!" I said.

Mandy and I were close in age. She was Aunt Tabby's daughter. Mandy has been here almost every day since Jessica's death. When I say that Mandy saved my life I mean that in every sense of the word. If she had not been here cracking silly jokes and rocking me in her arms I think that I would have died from a broken heart. I missed the hell out of Jessica.

"Where are you girls off to in such a hurry?" My mom asked.

"We are just going to get some ice cream." Mandy quickly uttered.

"Here's some money." Mom offered us.

"Thanks, mom." I squirmed.

"You are welcome. Be safe." Mom said, walking us to the door.

"Be good!" Aunt Tabby yelled after us.

"Okay!" We replied in unison.

"Can you tell me what's going on?" I pressed Mandy zooming down the street.

"I am in big trouble!" She informed me.

"What kind of trouble?" I turned the corner.

"I owe this drug dealer a lot of money!" Mandy wailed.

"Did you offer him some pussy to cover your debt?" I questioned her.

"Yeah, but he said he wanted his money and that he had free pussy at home," Mandy grumbled.

"Ahh, fuck, man! How much do you owe?" I exclaimed.

"$1000.00." Mandy stuttered.

"Is that all because that's not shit?" I questioned my cousin.

"It is when you don't have it!" Mandy sobbed.

"Cousin, stop crying. I got you." I told her.

I made a u-turn in the middle of the street and headed for the bank.

"Why are we at the bank?" Mandy asked me with a look of terror on her face.

"To get you the money to pay off your debt." I shook my head at her.

"Oh, thank goodness. I thought you were about to rob the bank." Mandy said with relief in her eyes.
"I would never do that. I have been to jail one time and I am never doing anything else to get myself incarcerated." I explained to her.
Okay!" She bellowed.
I went into the bank and withdrew the money that Mandy needed. When I came back she was standing outside pacing the parking lot.
"What's wrong with you?" I questioned her.
"Dud just called. He wants his money now or he's going to kill my father." Mandy said in a frightened voice.
"Calm down! Just give me his address so that we can end this shit." I bellowed.
We were now on the way to this Dud spot. I sent my mom my location in case things went left.
*

We drove to the northeast side of the city. It was a different world from where I come from. Trash lined the streets while young men stood on the street corners.
"Pull up in this driveway," Mandy instructed me.
A bald head guy wearing an 8 Ball jacket came running up to my vehicle.
"What can I help you with?" The stranger questioned me.
"I am looking for Dud?" I uttered.
"Dud? What do you want with Dud? He's a busy man and doesn't have time for little girls." The man yapped.
"Look, is he here or what? It's urgent!" I bellowed.
"Come this way." He stuttered.
Mandy and I followed him inside the building.
"What can you help me with?" Dud grumbled.

"Dud, it's me, Mandy! I have your money." She stammered.

He looked up and chuckled.

Dud was surprised that Mandy was able to come up with the money so quickly.

"Good! Now I won't have to kill your daddy." He cackled in an eerie voice.

I pulled the money from my purse and handed it over to him. I watched as he counted it twice.

"It's all there!" I exclaimed.

"I see. What's your name?" He questioned me.

"I am Dottie," I muttered.

"You are sexy as fuck! Do you have a man?" Dud questioned me.

"Nah, I am not interested in anyone." I retorted.

"Can I take you out sometime?" Dud asked me.

Mandy gave me a weird look.

"Please don't take it personally it's nothing against you but I don't date because I am in school. I am trying to get my doctorate in Business." I quickly explained.

"Hmm. Beauty and brains. I like that. Mandy, you need to take notes from your friend. Using drugs ain't good for you, baby girl." Dud retorted.

"This is my cousin." Mandy corrected Dud.

"Oh, my bad! The message is still the same: get your shit together, Mandy." Dud howled.

"Damn, I hear you!" Mandy sassed.

"This shit is not a game. There are so many pretty females strung out on shit. I don't want you to be one of those girls." Dud preached to Mandy.

"Thanks, I didn't know that you cared," Mandy replied.

"I am not the monster that you think that I am. Under all of this hardness, I am a nice guy. Get on the straight and narrow before it's too late to turn around." Dud advised Mandy.

"I will take everything that you are telling me under consideration." She bellowed.

"We have to go. It was great meeting you, Dud." I said turning to leave.

"Wait! I didn't get your name." Dud surprised me.

"I am Dottie." I spat.

"Dottie, take my number and call me whenever you want to take a break from all of the studying that has you so occupied." Dud grinned.

"I will do that." I smiled.

"Ladies be safe," Dud said walking us out of the building.

He stood in the entryway staring our way. Dud seemed to be overprotective over the things that he loved.

Drug dealers were not my thing but Dud seemed like he was cut from a different cloth. Maybe I will call him and maybe I won't. Only time will tell.

"Do you like him?" Mandy questioned me as I pulled out of the driveway.

"Who?" I replied, not knowing what she was talking about.

"Dud, silly! Who else?" Mandy pressed me.

"I am not sure but he seems alright," I said, putting on my seatbelt.

"I think that he likes you." She debates

"Look, can we not talk about Dud? Your debt is paid so let's just forget that this even happened." I concluded.

"Let's get some ice cream before we go back to the house," Mandy suggested.

"Ain't that where we told our moms we were going?" I laughed.

"Yes, we are something else!" I bellowed as I headed for the ice cream spot.

Chapter 16
Poker

I just dropped off my last customer for the day. I am a Lyft driver by day and a stripper by night. I hurried home to fry some chicken before dinner. I was thinking about making rice, peas, and cornbread with it. I noticed Nano's truck in my driveway.
"Hey, babe! How are you doing today?" I asked Nano.
"I am doing okay. These classes are kicking my ass though." Nano complained.
"Awe, babe, it will pay off in the end. I did something very rewarding today." I told him taking off my boots.
"What was that?" Nano asked me.
"I pressed your baby mama," I informed him.
"You did what?" Nano responded angrily.

"I called that bitch up and told her she needs to let you see London," I explained.

"Poker, I told you to leave this shit alone. I will handle Rhema when the time is right." Nano groaned.

"I know what you said but I just wanted to help. It isn't fair that you aren't allowed to see your daughter." I pouted.

"Stay out of this shit! It's nobody's fault but mine. I am the one that fucked up and that's why I can't see my daughter. Time will heal all of this." Nano expressed deep regret for his actions.

"Okay! I will stay out of you and your baby mama's shit." I bellowed.

"Thank you. So what's on the dinner menu?" He pressed me.

"Fried chicken, peas, and rice," I uttered.

"Ohh, I can't wait to eat." He grabbed me around my waist.

"I am about to get to cooking," I responded, kissing Nano passionately.

"Get to it then, lady!" Nano slapped me on my ass.

"Stop that before you eat something other than food. You are turning me the fuck on!" I cooed rubbing between my thighs.

"You look so hot right now but I would rather eat food than pussy because I don't have the energy needed to pound on your shit at the moment." Nano rubbed on his dick.

"Man oh, man! It's always been something with you since you started school again. You never want to fuck or do anything fun." I complained.

"When I have time you always have to work. Poker, we both have busy lives. I am content with the way things are for the time being. Sex isn't everything, trust me I know better than anyone." Nano piped.

"Whatever, read a book or something. I am wasting time fuckin with you. I need to cook so that I can eat and get my ass in bed." I frowned.

"I forgot that you have to work tonight." Nano sighed heavily.

*

I was preparing to cook dinner when I smelled something so stank that it made me gag. What the fuck is that? I walked into the living room and caught Nano smoking some shit that I knew wasn't reefer.

"What are you smoking?" I pressed him.

"K2!" He responded. coughing uncontrollably.

I went to the kitchen to get the fool a glass of water.

"You do know that shit is incense that you are smoking? I know a few niggas that ended up in the mental ward from smoking that shit." I warned him.

"Baby, I am good. Nah, I didn't know that. I don't know what they were smoking because it never happened to me." He uttered.

"Whatever happened to just smoking weed?" I questioned Nano.

I rather smoke this than get high on my supply." He retorted, taking a sip of water.

"Nano, you have so much to live for don't fuck it up by smoking this shit!' I bellowed.

"Poker, you are not my mother so stop trying to tell me what to do!" He yelled in frustration.

"I am not trying to be your mother!' I argued.

"Then stay the fuck out of my business!" He yelped.

His words hurt me to the core. I didn't have to put up with this at all. I was too pretty, too kind, and too cool to accept any kind of mess from any man.

"Look Nano, I think that you need to go home because I am not down with you smoking this shit in my place," I told him with my hands on my hips.

"Poker, I am sorry!" Nano pleaded.

"There is no need for you to be sorry because my decision has been made. I need you to leave now." I said calmly.

"Come on, give me another chance. Don't throw me out!" He spat.

"Listen, I am not Rhema. I don't give anybody second chances to mistreat me. Please get the fuck out!" I howled, holding the door open for him.

"Fuck you, Poker! I thought you were the one." He said with a mad face.

"Boy bye. You ain't saying nothing that I want to hear." I slammed the door.

Chapter 17
Nano

No woman had ever dumped me like this before without giving me a chance to do right. Poker had me fucked up in the head right now. I didn't love her at all. She was just my rebound bitch.
I missed Rhema so much and I wanted my old thing back but I was afraid to approach her because of her Uncle Bruno. I had to do something though.
I decided to call her up.
"Hello," Rhema answered.
"Baby, I miss you and London. Please come back home." I pressed her.
"Nano, are you out of your motherfuckin mind? I don't want your ass anymore. I have moved on and I suggest that you do the same!" Rhema bellowed.
I couldn't believe what I was hearing.

"Rhema, I know that you ain't been giving my pussy away!" I screamed into the phone.

"If I did it is not any of your damn business. The last time I checked this pussy was attached to my body and not yours. You weren't worried about it when you were fuckin Jessica in our bed so stop fuckin calling my damn phone." Rhema concluded by throwing the phone across the room.

This was not the way that I wanted our conversation to go. I had expected Rhema to take me back. My mood had gone sour. I had fucked up big time with Rhema. What am I going to do now?

I decided to call up one of my bitches. Sex always made me feel better.

"What's up?" I asked Angel.

"Nothing much." She replied.

"I want to do a little something with you," I stated.

"I need some money. I don't fuck for free." Angel declared.
"I know so are you going to let me hit it or not?" I pressed her.
"Sure, meet me at my place in fifteen minutes. I am about to blow your mind." Angel giggled.
"Who is that?" Sparkle asked Angel.
"Nano!" I laughed.
"Oh, he wants to misbehave!" Sparkle smirked.
"Must be. I am getting in the shower. Hold shit down for me in case that nigga decides to bring his ass early." Angel instructed Sparkle.
"Best friend, I will have his ass hot and ready fuck." Sparkle promised me.
"Do your thing, bestie, because we are about to get laid and paid tonight," I assured her.
*
Angel was a cool-ass bitch. We fucked around a few times before I

got with Rhema. She has a big ass and perky tits that I loved to tug.

I rang Angel's doorbell.

"Can I help you?" Sparkle opened the door wearing nothing but her birthday suit.

"I think that I have the wrong address." I turned around.

"Wait!" Sparkle yelped.

"What is it?" I barked.

"Are you looking for Angel?" Sparkle questioned me.

"Yes, I am!" I proudly muttered.

"Step right inside. Angel will be right down." Sparkle told me.

Who was this naked woman and why was she answering the door butt-ass naked?

"Where is Angel?" I asked, looking around.

"She's upstairs. Would you like a drink?" Sparkle asked me.

"I would love a cold beer," I replied.

When Sparkle returned with the beer she accidentally spilled it on my sweatpants.

"Oh, damn, my bad! Let me help you. " Sparkle bellowed.

The next thing that I knew was Sparkle was suckin my dick. I wanted to push her away but my body was going against my thoughts. I didn't know how I was going to explain this shit to Angel.

This bitch was suckin me so good that I cummed in her mouth twice already. I was ready to fuck and did not know what was taking Angel so damn long.

"Where's the bedroom?" I asked with bass in my voice.

"This way!" Sparkle eagerly took me by the hand.

Once in the bedroom, I pushed her onto the bed. Spreading her legs wide I entered her moist vagina.

"Ohhhh!" She delightfully squealed before wrapping her legs around my waist.

Her pussy was tight and fuckable. I loved every minute of being inside of her. Her soft moans made me pump even harder.

"Well, well, well. What do we have here?" Angel spat walking into the living room.

I spun around to see Angel standing near me.

"I can explain!" I retorted.

"You are funny, Nano. I set this whole thing up. I knew that you wouldn't be able to resist my best friend. You are a weak ass motherfucker!" Angel scolded me.

"This is so fucked up!" I grumbled.

"Shut up nigga! You are in my sex room. I make the motherfuckin rules here and you will comply. Say less and let's fuck!" Angel ordered me.

Chapter 18
Rhema
5 Months Later

Today was the grand opening of my beauty bar. It had cost me a pretty penny. I worked very hard to come up with the funds to purchase the building and everything that was inside. Uncle Bruno and Kossi matched me dollar for dollar. They did everything within their power to help me to succeed. Judah had my sign custom-made. *Glam Up With Rhema* was my beauty bar's name. I was so proud of my team and myself. Without Judah and Aunti Kossi and Uncle Bruno's help this just wouldn't have been possible so soon.

It had taken me months to get the shop the way that I had envisioned it. My blood, sweat, and tears were finally paying off.

"Congratulations," Ghera happily announced walking into the shop.
"Ghera! What are you doing here?" I retorted.
"I saw your grand opening sign. I came to get my lashes done. I heard that you were the best in the town." Ghera bellowed.
I laughed.
"What's so funny?" Ghera asked me.
Nothing. I am so happy. I have my beauty bar and a new man. I owe it all to you." I embraced Ghera.
"Rhema, you deserve all of this and much more." I am proud of you. Ghera spat.
"Ghera, I want to thank you," I told her.
"For what? I didn't do a thing." Ghera chirped.
"Yes, you did! Do you remember that day at the mall?" I questioned her.
"Vaguely!" She bellowed.

"On that day you encouraged me to do better for myself and London. I owe you an apology. I made myself look like a fool. I should have never pressed you the way that I did about Nano. I am glad that I did though. You overlooked all the bad in me and poured into me as every woman should do to another." I smiled.
"I was only trying to help. You seemed very unhappy. I just wanted you to know that I wasn't sleeping with Nano." Ghera sighed.
"I know that now. have a seat over here so I can get you out of here. Since you are my first customer, your services are free." I grinned.
"Wow! Today must be my lucky day." Ghera retorted.
Today was a very busy day for me. I am so glad that I hired a few ladies to help out. I knew that I couldn't do everything myself especially when ladies were steadily walking in

without appointments.

"Rhema, I am starving and it's hot in here. When are we gonna get a break." Ginger complained.

"When you are done with your client, take an hour's break," I instructed her.

"What about us?" Paris muttered with a pained look on her face.

"I was talking about everyone." I smiled at Paris.

"Okay!" She smiled back after getting back to work.

My stomach was touching my back as well. I was ready to eat myself. I wanted some good ole soul food.

"I am looking for Rhema!" A delivery guy grumbled.

"I am she." I blurted.

"I have a delivery for you. Can you sign here?" I grunted.

"I hope someone sent some food. I am making sure that I pack a lunch and some snacks tomorrow!" Yolanda yapped.

"I am with you on that, girl." I spat.

Someone had sent us pizza and wigs. I was so happy. I bet it was Judah. He was always surprising me.

"Can we eat now?" Paris pleaded with me.

"Only if our clients agree to eat with us," I told her.

"That food smells good. I want in." Mary agreed.

"I have to be to work soon but fuck that I am gonna be late today!" Janice jumped from the styling to wash her hands.

We got back to business as usual after stuffing our faces. No one complained about anything.

My phone rang.

"Hello," I answered.

"I hope you and your beauty crew enjoyed lunch!" Judah piped.

"Thank you! I knew it was you, babe, that sent all of this food. It was delicious." I replied amused.

"Great, I just wanted to make sure that you all had eaten. I know how hard you all work." Judah chuckled.

*

It was now closing time. We were tidying up. I only accepted cards as payment because it lessened my chances of getting robbed. All of the funds that I earned went straight to the bank. I took every precaution that I could to keep myself and my crew safe.

"I am tired. Are you all ready to go yet?" I asked the ladies.

"I just need to finish getting this trash up and then we can go," Paris uttered.

"My ride's here so I am about to bounce," Yolanda told me.

"See you tomorrow," I yelled after her.

Chapter 19
Dottie

"Ohh, Dud, that feels so good!" I screamed while he fucked me from the back.

Who would have thought that doggie style would be my favorite sexual position? I could feel every inch of Dud's dick. Each time that we fucked it was like I was on a natural high. I just couldn't get enough.

I couldn't get the man off my mind so I decided to give him a chance. Here I am months later getting more dick than the law allowed.

Someone was knocking on Dud's apartment door. He kept fuckin me like no one existed in this shady-ass world but us.

"Boss, we have a problem!" Otis screamed through the door.

"Whatever it is, handle it! I am busy with my woman." Dud snarled.

Bae, handle your business. I am tired anyways." I sighed heavily.

"Are you sure about that?" he questioned me as someone kicked the door.

"Of course, I need to study. I am okay." I reassured him.

"See that's why I love you so much. You are so understanding and you don't nag me." Dud kissed me passionately.

"That's because you treat me well," I smirked.

"I am going to always do good by you, Dot. You are an amazing woman and lover. I am never going to let you go." Dud declared.

"I hope that's a promise and not something that you tell all the girls after you get between their legs." I retorted.

"I am a grown man and I can admit to the shit that I have done. I ain't never told any woman what I just

said to you. None of them has ever made me feel complete the way that you do." Dud said through his tears.
"Don't cry!" I pleaded.
I felt bad for putting him on the spot like that.
"I am not crying!" He lied.
"Awe," I embraced him tightly.
*
I took a quick shower before leaving. I didn't want to go home looking like I just got fucked. My parents would have a fit if they knew that I had a drug-swingling boyfriend. I would probably never live it down. I loved Dud and even if my parents found out about our relationship I would not let him go.
*
"Where have you been?" Nina barked at me.
"I was out with a friend," I told her.
Mom was crying. I haven't seen her this distraught since Jessica died.

"Why didn't you answer your phone?" Nina nagged at me.

"Mom, I am 24 years old and I am not a child. I turned my phone off because I didn't want to be disturbed." I muttered.

Damn. What was her problem tonight? Every night it was something and I was so tired of the shit.

"I have looked everywhere and still can't find her!" Aunt Tabby fumed when she entered the house.

"What's going on?" I was confused.

"I haven't seen Mandy in a few days! Her phone is going straight to voicemail. Something is wrong, I just know it." Auntie Tabby screeched.

I grabbed my car keys and headed for the door.

"Where are you going?" Nina asked me.

"To bring Mandy home," I concluded walking out the door.

I didn't know where to start looking for Mandy but I knew that she wouldn't be in my neck of the woods. Mandy loved the hood. Everything about the hood screamed her name. I decided to hit Dud's line to tell him what was going on.

"Yo! Dud answered.

"Bae, what are you doing?" I asked him.

"I am handling some important business. Why what's up? I can sense some urgency in your voice." Dud questioned me.

"Mandy is missing and I believe that she's in some serious trouble," I informed him.

"What the fuck is little cousin into now?" Dud snarled.

"A few weeks ago she told me that she was fuckin around with BJ and his gang. They are notorious for drugs, and turning bitches out." I explained to my man.

"EHH, so you think one of those niggas done turned her out and has her tricking out here in these streets?" He questioned me through clenched teeth.

I could tell that Dud was getting mad as hell. He cared for Mandy because she was my family. Anything that I loved he loved and vice versa.

"It's a hunch and if that's true Mandy is trapped with those assholes. There is no telling what they are doing to her.. Those niggas won't let her go especially if she's their money maker." I angrily spat.

"You are right! They probably introduced her to heroin or some wild shit by now. I am going to head over there with my crew. If she's there I am knocking niggas the fuck out. If I have to, I will kill them. Don't worry about a motherfuckin thing because I am bringing Mandy home." Dud retorted.

Chapter 20
Mandy

I made a bad decision when I decided to go to the bar with BJ and his boys. I thought it would be cool to party with them but boy was I wrong. Everything went well that night. BJ bought the bar out so I was drunk as hell. I danced the night away with different men. It was fun. I felt amazing like nothing in the world mattered but what was happening at the moment.
I woke up hours later with some creep on top of me.
"Get the fuck off of me!" I let out a terrified scream.
This man was taking advantage of me. I had never been raped before. I was trying to figure out where the hell I was at. Nothing seemed familiar and the more that I screamed the worse the pain got. I

didn't know what kind of dick this guy had but it was killing my insides. "Shut up and take this dick, bitch! I paid for this pussy and I am not going to let you go until I get my money's worth." The rapist raged. "Paid for pussy! I didn't consent to this!" I screamed.

The more I screamed and fought the rougher the crazy dude became.

I didn't know what else to do but to lay here. I prayed that it would be over soon.

He finished by spilling his semen on my face. I have never felt more humiliated in my life. I felt so many emotions. I was happy that he was finished but angry that he thought that it was okay to rape me. I watched him as he pulled his black trousers up. I noticed a tattoo of a scorpion on his left thigh. I made a mental note of it. This asshole will pay for what he has done to me.

"Until next time, sugar!" He bellowed, tipping his hat as he left the room.
I was so glad that he was gone.
I stood up. I tried to walk but my legs were wobbly.
"Come on Maddy, you can do this," I told myself.
I turned the doorknob and that's when I discovered that I was locked inside. I started pounding at the door with my fist but no one answered.
What the fuck is going on?

*

"What are we going to do with Mandy? We can't keep her cooped up in the little room like that. What if someone comes snooping around here looking for her?" Adrienne pressed BJ.
"Man, look, nobody's gonna be looking for that smoked-out bitch. Stop worrying so much. I am handling the situation." BJ retorted.

"You better because I will not go down for this!" Adrienne bellowed.
Adrienne wasn't sure that her brother knew what he was talking about. Mandy wasn't your typical smoker from the hood. She had a good loving family who loved her very much. Trouble was brewing so she decided to get the hell out of dodge. Adrienne was tired of these sticky situations that she always found herself in whenever her brother came around.
Adrienne packed up her things which she didn't have much. She had just come from Jamaica. To stay out of bullshit she decided to catch the next flight out.
"Where are you going?" BJ questioned Adrienne.
"I have a modeling gig in Jamaica. I just got the call so you are on your own with this crazy shit!" Adrienne lied to her brother.

"Who is going to keep an eye on this little bitch now! Fuck, I am not built for this shit." BJ screeched.

"Let her go then. It's the only advice that I can give you." Adrienne suggested.

She just wasn't down with any of this crazy shit.

"I might have to do just that! Mandy was supposed to be my money moneymaker." BJ complained.

"I am telling you this because I love you. Blood is thicker than water but bro, this ain't the way to come up. Would you want some bitchass niggas doing this to me?" Adrienne argued.

"Hell no! What kind of question is that? I would come for every one of those niggas with guns blasting." BJ pounded one fist into the other palm.

"There is your answer. Be a good man, like mama and daddy raised you to be. I have to go now, Bro. See you when I get back." Adrienne embraced her brother tightly.

Little did BJ know but this was the last time that he would ever see his baby sister. Adrienne had made up her mind to never return to the states. She knew that her brother would never change his evil ways and couldn't bear to watch him die by the sword.

Now that Adrienne was gone he called his crew to the house. He wanted to let Mandy go but he needed help.

Bruce, a heavy-set but muscular dude, arrived at the spot first. "What do you need, boss?' Bruce looked at his watch.

"Let's wait for the others to arrive," BJ muttered.

"Boss, I don't have all day. Today is my daughter's birthday party. If I

miss it, that's going to be my ass on the line. There is no telling when these niggas going to come through. Just tell me what needs to be done and I will fix it." Bruce pressed me.
"Your woman is ruling you like that! Shit, it must be love." BJ chuckled.
"Yeah, nigga, I love her and I am not trying to lose her. What's good?" Bruce uttered.
"Hey, what's poppin'? I was on my way here when I received the emergency group text." Juke yelped walking in the door with a duffle bag full of money.
He handed BJ the duffle bag that contained the cash from the drug deal with the Murdaugh brothers. BJ looked inside.
"How was the drop?" BJ questioned Juke.
Everything went very smoothly. I was in and out of that motherfucker in a flash." Juke grunted.

"Wonderful! I got some shit for ya to handle. Bruce is in a hurry so he can't wait for the others." BJ chuckled as he explained.

*

I was so scared. I couldn't figure out how I got here. I searched the room for my phone but couldn't find it. Fuck! All I remembered was partying and getting fucked up. I hoped that my parents were looking for me. My body ached badly from that creep raping me. I swear that if I get out of this mess alive that I am going to change my whole life. I am not about this life. Suddenly two men busted through the door. I didn't get a chance to get a good look at them. One put a pillowcase or something over my head. I tried to fight them but they were very strong.

"Chill, shorty, we are letting you go!" Juke huffed.

Those words gave me so much life.

They put me into a vehicle. They drove me around for a while before stopping. The back seat door opened. One of the guys helped me out.
"Count to 100 before taking the bag off. If you don't we will kill you and serve your head on a platter to your parents. Do you understand?" Bruce yelled in an evil voice at me.
"Yes!" I said in a frightened voice.
"Don't fuck up because we have eyes and ears everywhere!" He declared.
I heard them drive off. I didn't wait to count to 100. I ran as fast as I could in the other direction. I was not a fool, I knew that I had to get myself some help quickly.
I didn't recognize my surroundings and no one was around. I kept running until I ran into a woman.

Help me! Someone kidnapped me. I was raped, please." I screamed in terror.

I kept looking behind because I was afraid those men would come back to hurt me.

"Calm down! Come with me. What's your name?" The lady questioned me.

The woman dragged me behind a building because she didn't want to attract the wrong attention to us.

"Mandy Mitchum. Can I use your phone to call my mom? I am sure that she's very worried about me.

"First, I need you to pull yourself together. I am going to call the police and then you can call your mom. My name is Cherry." She said, handing me a soda from her bag.

"Please, don't call the police, they already threatened to kill me. I just want to go home and forget all of this has happened.

"It's your choice. I am very sorry that those men violated you. I am certain that you didn't deserve any of it. Go ahead and call your mom." Cherry instructed me.

*

Tabby waited patiently at Nina's for Dottie to call with news of Mandy.
"Hello," Tabby answered her phone.
"Mom, can you come to get me?" I wailed into the phone.
"Are you, okay? Yes, I am coming now! Where are you?" Tabby badgered me with questions.
"No, I was raped. I am Duckberry road." I told my mom.
"Nina and I are on the way." Tabby grabbed her keys and ran out the door with Nina behind her.
"Okay, mom," I concluded.

*

Nina decides to call Dottie to let her know that they were on the way to get Mandy.

"Did she say anything else?" Dottie yelled.
"No, baby!" Nina yelped.
"Okay, mom, I will meet you back at the house," Dottie concluded.
"What happened?" Dud impatiently asked me.
"She was kidnapped and raped. Some niggas had her locked in a room." Dottie explained.
"Sounds like Mandy was being sex trafficked. I wonder what made her kidnappers let her go?" Dud fumed.
"God heard my prayers." I smiled.
"That's because you are a God-fearing woman." Dud retorted.
"I am going to the house. I will see you later." Dottie smiled at him.
"Those niggas are lucky that I didn't catch them with Mandy because there would have been a lot of bloodsheds." Dud huffed.
"I don't want blood on your hands." Dottie spat.

*

"Dottie!" Mandy ran straight to me when she walked inside the house. "It's so good to see you, alive!" I bellowed with tears in my eyes embracing my cousin.

"It's good to be back with my family. I swear that I am giving up partying. This was a wake-up call for me so I am done with drinking and the drugs. Someone raped me and it was all of my faults because I had no business partying with BJ and his crew." Mandy informed with tears in her eyes.

"What is she talking about?" Tabby glared at Nina.

"Our children are not perfect and they must live their lives and learn from their actions. Instead of being angry about Mandy's truth, be happy that she's not 6ft under and is willing to change her actions. Jessica won't ever get that chance to right her wrongs in life." Nina expressed to her sister Tabby.

"I am sorry, mommy. I was just doing me and I thought that partying with those dope boys was the way to go. I found out the wrong way that it isn't. This will never happen to me again." I promised.

"Oh, I am just happy that you are alive!" Tabby exclaimed.

"I just want a hot shower and some clean clothes." I retorted.

"Come with me, Mandy. I will make sure you are straight." Dottie spat leading the way.

Once upstairs Dottie closed and locked her bedroom door.

"I want to kill those motherfuckers for what they did to me. I thought that they were my friends!" I wept uncontrollably.

"I understand. BJ and his niggas are some wild motherfuckers." Dottie fumed.

Chapter 21
Zaria

I have been seeking counseling because I can't sleep at night since Jessica's murder. I swear that her death hit me deep within my soul.
Therapy was going well and my anxiety has improved a great deal. I have been keeping my ass in the house. Catering to my man was not a bad thing after all. Terrell was so good to me.
Today I wanted to get my hair done. My sister Raquel had made our appointments at a new shop that we heard did good hair, nails, and lashes.
"Honey, can I have some money? Raquel and I are having a beauty day." I asked my husband.
"Sure, here's $500.00. I knew that you would be needing to get your hair and stuff done." Terrell chuckled.

"Thank you, babe!" I squealed.
"It's no problem. I love to make you happy. Have a great day with Raquel. I need to run before I am late for work." Terrell rushed out of the door.
I cleaned up the kitchen. I made breakfast for my husband and myself. When I was done I called up Raquel.
"Hey, sis!" Raquel answered.
"Terrell gave me some money so you don't have to spend your hard-earned money on me!" I bellowed.
"That's wonderful, sis, but this our beauty sis day, and it's on me. Buy yourself a new Fendi bag or something." Raquel insisted.
"Are you sure, sis?" I protested.
"Sis, if you don't stop I am going to hit you upside your head. Recognize a blessing when you are receiving one." Raquel scolded me.

"Oh, I don't want that!" I spat.
"Now that we have that handled, what time will you be ready for me to scoop you?" Raquel questioned me.
"I need to shower and throw the laundry in the dryer so I will say a half hour tops," I informed my sister.
"I will be there in twenty so your ass better be out of the shower by then. I need to drop Rex to the groomers so I will be early." Raquel sighed.
"I promise, so do what you need to do because I am about to hop in the shower now. I hope that you got that nasty dog in his cage because I hate dog hair." I bellowed.
"Yes, he has his wild ass in his cage or he wouldn't be in my truck." Raquel laughed at me.
"Okay, sis. I will see you in a little bit." I grinned.

*

We walked into the beauty shop. It was a quaint little spot.

"We are here for our appointments," Raquel announced to the receptionist.

"What are your names?" The receptionist asked without looking up from her laptop.

"Zaria and Raquel." My sister uttered politely.

"Oh, it's you!" The receptionist looked up at me and snarled.

To my surprise, it was Shana, TJ's mama.

"Zaria, who is this rude ass bitch!" Raquel asked me, taking off her earrings.

One thing about my big sister is she doesn't play when it comes to me. Raquel is always already to fuck somebody up about me.

"That's nobody!" I glared at Shana.

"I am Shana! You are a nobody ass bitch!" Shanan nastily retorted.

Pow!

Raquel slapped Shana across the face. I pulled her across the desk and then we pounded and stomped her ass.

"I told your ass to stop disrespecting me. I am Terrell's wife now! I am not going no fuckin where so you might as well get used to it cause if not I am beating your ass every chance that I get." I howled before dumping her coffee on her fuckin head.

"Oh, I see this is the bitch that keeps fuckin with you!" Raquel snarled.

"Yep, but I am done being nice. Today is the last day for that." I stammered as I regained my composure.

"What the hell is going on in here?" Rhema screamed.

When I noticed it was Rhema, I punched her dead in her mouth.

"I don't want my hair done here," I told Raquel.

Rhema pulled out her weapon on me.

This bitch has a gun!" Raquel shrieked.

"She's going to have to kill us because we are leaving. All she does is pull guns out on people like she's tough or some shit. This is the crazy bitch who killed Jessica so she had that shit coming!" I howled.

"Fuck you, Zaria!" Rhema screeched. "I will let you have that only because you have that gun. I have a husband and a stepson to live for. Another time and another place your ass would be mine.

Here's some advice: get better help because Shana ain't shit!" I retorted.

"Go to hell!" Shana screamed at me.

"Raquel, let's go. We shouldn't argue with fools." I declared.

"I agree!" Raquel bellowed following me out of the shop.

"Raquel, I can't take your ass anywhere." I retorted.

Chapter 22
BJ
A Month Later

I was trying to think of some new ways to make more money. The economy was fucked so that meant that I had to spend more money on everything. I was having trouble making ends meet. My men wanted more money for the services that they provided to me. I couldn't just up and fire them because they knew everything about my empire. They were ten toes deep in all the shit. We built this shit with our blood, sweat, and tears. It would be a disaster if I tried to lay them off. We were family so I had to find a way to make things right.

"BJ, I think I have an idea to help solve your money problems!" Duke bellowed.

"What's that, Partner?" I asked excitedly.

Okay, well you know that spot where we used to make all our drug deals when we first started? It's for sale. I was thinking that you could make it an offer and turn it into a Sports bar. You could sell wings and have a fish fry every Friday. People will come and then have happy hours on the weekdays but on the weekend we will have the spot jumping. Charge the patrons $15 before ten and $30 after." Duke suggested.

"Yeah, that sounds like a great idea. I wonder how much the spot is going for." I mumbled.

"I am not sure but we can find out. I saw this fine ass real estate lady putting up a sign over there. She gave me her business card." Duke informed me.

"Where is it?" I stammered.

"Right, here!" Juke pulled the card out of his wallet.
I looked the card over.
"I am going to call this Madison Brooks." I mumbled.
"Great but listen to my other money making ideas first." He bellowed.
"Okay, I am listening." I stuttered and took a seat in my recliner.
"So the building on Arnett and Rugby is for sale." Duke stalked off but I interrupted him.
"Are you talking about the corner store that sold penny cookies and candy back in the day?" I questioned Duke.
"Yes, remember when arcade games used to be in the store?
"Yes, I used to have an awesome time playing those arcade games. Those were the good ole days for sure." I chuckled.

"A fortune could be made in the store by making cold and hot subs, chicken wings, etc. You could get your liquor license and sell beer and cigarettes. if you get all the household and personal accessories people will come and buy you out. Get the weave and things that women like and they will be running in and out the store all day long. Get your lottery license and watch grandma and grandpa come limping in there buying up all of those scratch offs." Duke told me scratching his head.
"You are right and then if we accept food stamps we could make even more. Nigga, you are smart as fuck! You should become a mentor. I am sure you could make shit loads of money helping niggas figure out their lives." I chuckled.
"Maybe, I might take your advice if life gets too much for me." Duke grinned at me.

"I am going to make some phone calls. I will let you know what I come up with. Thanks, Duke." I announced with excitement.

*

Mandy was sick to her stomach. She didn't know what was wrong with her so she decided to make a doctor appointment. Mandy thought she had the flu or covid.
"Where are you going?" Tabby asked her.
"To the doctor." Mandy sulked.
"Oh, sweetheart, I didn't know that you were still feeling down. Let me accompany you to your appointment." Tabby suggested.
Mandy really didn't want her mom to come with her but to keep the peace she allowed Tabby to come with her. Mandy just felt like a small child when she was around her mother. The nurse had Mandy piss in a cup. She also took some blood from her.

Dr. Conner entered the room. "Mandy, I understand that you are not feeling very well." Dr. Conner questioned me.

"No, I am very nauseous and feeling tired all the time no matter how much I rest." I explained.

"Uh Huh, I have gone over your test results and I believe that I know what's causing all of these issues." Dr. Conner grinned at me.

I didn't know why he was grinning at me and I wasn't amused at all.

"Oh, okay! Please, tell me that I am not dying." I pleaded.

"Dying? What would make you think that you are dying?" The Doctor chuckled.

"What's wrong with my child?" Tabby shrieked.

Mandy hung her head down low. She was scared to hear the doctor's diagnosis.

"Mandy, you are pregnant!" He revealed.
"Pregnant? I can't be pregnant!" Mandy screamed.
Mandy began throwing things around the room. She had a big ole hissy fit.
Once the nurses calmed Mandy down. Dr. Conner came back into the room to complete our visit.
"Mandy, I have never seen anyone react the way you just did when they learned that they were pregnant. Can you please explain to me what's going on with you?" Dr. Connor questioned me.
"I am pregnant by my rapist!" Mandy bellowed.
Tabby and Dr. Connor looked very shocked and was at a loss of words.
The doctor referred Mandy to see a therapist. He also suggested that she have an abortion but Mandy was against abortions. Mandy felt like her son or daughter deserved a chance

in life even if the dad is an asshole.
"With God we will get through this!" Tabby wailed.
"Ma, will you stop crying, damn! I am going through a lot right now. I can't think of you carrying on like this." Mandy frowned.
"I am sorry but I am your mother and can't always contain my feelings." Tabby concurred.
"I am sorry, ma. I didn't mean to yell at you. I am so irritated right now. I just want those men to pay for what they did to me." Mandy apologized.
"It's okay, sweetheart, when you hurt I feel your pain." Tabby retorted.
"No doubt!" Mandy claimed.

*

Later at Mandy's Auntie Nina's house

When Mandy and Tabby arrived Mandy greeted her Auntie Nina and Uncle Harold with hugs and kisses before dashing to Dottie's bedroom.

"Bae, I need to go, Mandy just entered my bedroom." Dottie explained to Dud.

"Okay, tell Mandy hello. Make sure to call me later." He concluded.

What's up, cousin?" Dottie happily squealed.

"We have a lot to discuss. I am so annoyed." Mandy told Dottie.

"Have a seat and tell me what's on your mind." Dottie insisted.

Mandy loved her cousin Dottie because she would drop everything in a heartbeat just to make sure that she was good.

"I went to the doctor today." Mandy stated, hanging my head down low.

"What happened? Hold your head up so I can look you in your face." Dottie uttered.

"I am pregnant!" Mandy exclaimed.

"You are what? How, who have you been getting dick from?" Dottie badgered Mandy with questions.

"I ain't been getting dick. I was raped remember?" Mandy unhappily retorted.

"OMG! I am so sorry. What are you going to do about it? You can't keep it, you know that?" Dottie said in a frustrated manner.

"I will not abort my child! My baby deserves a chance at life no matter how he or she was conceived." Mandy blurted loudly.

"If that's what you want then I will be standing right by your side." Dottie promised, embracing Mandy. The hug felt so amazing to Mandy and it eased her fears.

"What I want is for those motherfuckers to pay for what they did to me. My rapist needs to go down for this." Mandy fumed.

"How will we find out who he is?" Dottie questioned Mandy.

"I never told you or anyone else this but my rapist has a tattoo of a scorpion on his left thigh." Mandy revealed.
"Interesting, come with me!" Dottie bellowed.
"Where are we going?" Mandy protested because she wasn't in the mood to be hanging out.
"To see Dud so that he can handle this situation for us. We cannot handle this by ourselves." Dottie explained to me.
"Where are you girls going?" Nina bellowed.
"Out! We will be back." Dottie told her mom, pulling Mandy out the door behind her.
"Why were you so rude to Auntie?" Mandy asked Dottie.
"Because we are grown and shouldn't have to answer to anyone. It's not like we won't be back later." Dottie told Mandy.

Chapter 23
Dud

I was making myself a sandwich when Mandy and Dottie walked in my door. I knew something had to be up because Dottie never brought anyone to my pad with her.

"Hello, ladies, what brings you both to my crib?" I questioned them.

"Dud, Mandy is pregnant by her rapist!" Dottie bellowed.

"What?" I angrily yelped.

This has to be the worst news that I have heard all day.

"You heard Dottie. I am pregnant and I want those idiots to pay for all the pain that they caused me." Mandy claimed.

"Okay, BJ and his men have something to do with this crazy shit so we must go after them. Do you know who the rapist is?" I drilled Mandy.

I needed all the information that I could get to make this shit that's about to go down run as smoothly as possible.

"No, but he has a tattoo of a scorpion on his left thigh." Mandy reported.

"He shouldn't be hard to find because that's a very unusual tat for a black man." I explained.

"Awesome, so what's the next step?" Mandy eagerly asked me.

"Go home and wait for my call. I am going to end all of this shit tonight." I clasped my hands together.

It was time for war.

"Alright! Come on, let's go back to the house." Dottie told me.

Mandy didn't want to leave. She wanted to be there to see those men suffer for what they did to her.

"I want to help!" Mandy protested.

"Allow me to handle this. It's going to be very dangerous and you will only distract me." I insisted.

*

My crew and I came up with a plan to surprise BJ and his team. We needed to catch them off guard. We decided to approach BJ's property after dark because most of his team or all should be gone home for the night. I took a group of twenty loyal men with me. Some kept an eye on the road and others surrounded the outside of the property. I took Sampson, Nekari, Polo, Magnum, and Paul inside the building with me. We had an arsenal of weapons on us and back up men close by on alert.

Nekari kicked in BJ's door. He was sleeping on the couch.

"What do you, nigga's want?" BJ growled.

Polo and Magnum had their weapons drawn at BJ's head.

"Who is the nigga that raped Mandy!" I howled.

"I don't know what the hell that you are talking about?" BJ lied.

"I am going to ask you one more motherfuckin 'time before having Sampson shoot you in one of your knee caps. Who in the fuck raped my cousin Mandy?" I screeched.

"Okay, okay! Please don't kill me." BJ squealed like a bitch.

"Talk to me!" I yelled.

I was tired of talking to this clown.

"It was Nano!" BJ yelled back.

"Kill this sorry piece of shit!" I ordered.

Boom.

"One shot to the motherfuckin 'head Your turn Magnum." Polo chuckled.

Boom.

"He's gone for good!" Magnum reported.

"Awesome, clean this shit up so we can find Nano's ass." I growled with authority.

Nano

Three weeks ago Poker came to the crib to inform me that she was pregnant. I was so fuckin happy. I stopped smoking that K2 shit because that was one the biggest issues in our relationship. I even buckled down and was well on my way to graduating in a few months. Everything was going so well.

"Baby, I am going to take a shower. Will you be ready for bed by the time I am finished?" Poker asked me.

"Nah, but I will be ready for some pussy when you are done." I chuckled.

"Boy, bye." Poker giggled twisting her phat ass towards the stairwell.

Suddenly, we heard pounding on the door.

"What the fuck is that?" I whispered to Poker.

"How should I know?" Poker panic.

"Hide!" bellowed but before either of them could make a move ten men with masks had entered.

"Oh my God, bae! Is this a home invasion?" Poker dropped to her knees in terror when Sampson stuck a gun to her fuckin head.

"She's pregnant! Leave her alone. I am sure it's probably me that you want. I don't have any money or drugs in the house." I informed the men.

"We don't want money!" Dud stammered.

"What do you want then?" I questioned them.

"I want you to strip so that I can see if you are the right person." Dud spat.

"Look, don't humiliate me like this." I pleaded.

Shut the fuckup and do as I say!" Dud thundered.

I really felt some type of way about this shit but there wasn't anything that I could do about it. I decided to cooperate. I pulled down my basketball shorts.

I noticed the man staring at my tat. I had a feeling that I wouldn't live to see tomorrow.

"So you love raping women?" Dud nastily spat at me.

"No, I never raped nobody!" I angrily defended myself.

"My baby cousin says differently. You are her rapist and this tattoo of the scorpion proves it." Dud calmly explained.

"I don't know what you are talking about!" I yelped.

"Nigga, you out here raping bitches when you got all of this ass and pussy at home! What the fuck is wrong with you?" Poker shouted at me.

"Baby, I never raped anyone in my fuckin life! Please, believe me." I shouted back.
"I don't believe you. You are a lying motherfucka. Stop fuckin lying to me and these men. They wouldn't be here if your victim hadn't told them about that fuckin tat." Poker hollered at me.
"She's pregnant you know!" Dud grinned.
"You fucked that lady raw! I am through with you." Poker cried out in disbelief.
"Who is pregnant?" I huffed.
I didn't know what the fuck this nigga was talking about. I had fucked so many broads so I wasn't being funny at all.
"Her name is Mandy, don't you know her?" Dud pressed me.
"Nah, I don't know that bitch!" I said in my mad voice.

Dud didn't like the way that Nano was playing on his intelligence. Dud gave Magnum and Polo one look and they both pulled the trigger at the same time.

"Clean this shit up!" Dud retorted.

The men went straight to work. Dud went outside to call Mandy and Dottie.

*

"Baby, what's happening?" Dottie pressed me.

"It's done. Tell Mandy not to stress over the bullshit anymore. I want her to focus on having a healthy child." I informed Dottie.

"I will. Thanks so much, baby!" Dottie exclaimed.

Dottie was proud to have a soldier like Dud on her team. Dud wasn't like other guys that she had been in relationships with. Dud was someone that she could count on.

Chapter 24
Rhema

Kossi woke me up out of my sleep to tell me the news of Nano's death. I couldn't believe that someone had murdered him and his new bitch. "Kossi, London doesn't have Nano anymore. She loved him dearly." I wept.

"I know that she did. I thought that you and Nano would work things out so that he could start spending time with London." Kossi muttered, shaking her head.

"Yeah, me too. I guess none of it was meant to be. I am so glad that I dodged that bullet because if I had stayed with Nano and put up with all of his bullshit it could have easily been me and London dead beside him." I thanked my lucky stars.

"Thank God for discernment!" Kossi shouted.

"It wasn't easy to leave him alone. I truly loved Nano but when I realized that the love wasn't being reciprocated I was so sad and lonely. I had to take a good look at my situation and that's when all at once I knew that the love that he was giving to me was not for me." I wiped my tears away with my bed sheet.

"Oh, baby! Auntie, is so sorry that you had to endure so much hurt and pain from a man that you loved with your whole heart." Kossi embraced me tightly.

"Thankfully, I have Judah in my life. I am so comfortable with him. I never have to second guess myself about anything when it comes to him." I smiled.

Whenever I thought of Judah, I felt so good. He was a good man to me and I felt so blessed to have him in London and my life.

*

A week Later

It was the day of Nano's wake. I had purchased London and myself matching mother and daughter black dresses and shoes. I wasn't going to attend the funeral because I don't want to put myself or London through anything that was unnecessary. London was too young to understand what was going on so what was the use?
Kossi and Bruno wanted to pay their respects so they were attending the wake as well.

*

"Is Rhema bringing my grandbaby?" Doris asked Kinena.
"Yes, mama. Give her some time to get here." Kinena assured her mother.
"She better or I will have a bone to pick with her later" Doris retorted.

"Mom this isn't the time or the place for nonsense. My brother is laying up front in a casket!" Kinena whimpered.

*

When we got to the funeral home I was surprised to see Judah waiting at the door. Judah never ceases to amaze me.

"Baby, what are you doing here?" I stammered.

"I am here to support you and London. What kind of man would I be to allow you to go through this terrible event alone." Judah took London into his arms.

"Wow!" I was amazed.

I headed straight for Nano's casket. I wasn't here to make friends or to smile in people faces who were fake as fuck on any other day. I wasn't with any nonsense for today. I just wanted to see Nano's body and leave

that's it. Nothing more or nothing less.
"Daddy!" London giggled when she saw her father in the casket.
"He's gone to live with the angels." I explained it to my daughter.
London kept on smiling.
"Who is this man that you have holding my granddaughter!" Doris fumed, glaring at me.
"This is Judah, my man." I happily announced.
"How dare you bring this nigga up in here disrespecting my dead son!" Doris hotly spewed at me.
"Wait a minute, Doris, get out of my niece's face before I knock your ass the fuck out!" Kossi fumed.
"Ladies, that's enough! I will leave this because all of this confusion is unnecessary." Judah tried to defuse the situation by handing London to me.

"If Judah is not welcome then neither am I!" I loudly blurted.

Mom, what have you done?" Kinena screamed at Doris.

"What's right!" Doris claimed.

"Nano, wouldn't want this. Mom, Nano had a good heart." Kinena bellowed.

"This tramp was never good enough for Nano!" Doris thundered.

"Wait a fuckin minute, Doris you don't know what you are talking about. Nano, cheated on me numerous times. He gave me std's and all so don't you dare call me out my name ever again in your life. Actually, your son was not good enough for me. He chose whores over me and his daughter." I retorted, walking away.

I didn't give a damn about what else Doris or anybody else in Nano's family had to say about me. I was free from his ass and his miserable ass mother.

*

Judah

I didn't like the way things went at the wake. I had a few things that I wanted to say in Rhema's defense but I left things alone.
I loved Rhema and London. They brought so much joy to my life. I bought a ring the other day because I wanted to propose to Rhema. I wanted her and London to be in my life permanently. Rhema and I had never been intimate. I didn't want her to become just another woman that I had fucked. She was special to me and I wanted to make her my wife. A woman like Rhema is very hard to find.
We drove back to Kossi's in silence. I was getting nervous because Rhema

had never been this quiet around me before.
"What's wrong, my love?" I questioned Rhema.

"I'm not proud of what happened at the funeral home." Rhema wept.
"Don't cry! London's grandmother may believe that I came to disrespect her dead son but that's far from the truth. I am not that kind of man. I can't help what she believes." I sighed heavily.
"I know, honey! I just want peace in my life. I am tired of all the drama." Rhema wiped her nose with a tissue.
"I just want to bring you happiness. I never want to let you down." I poured my heart out to Rhema.
I loved her so much. I never wanted to cause her any hurt or pain.`
"I feel you. Judah, you have made the happiest woman in the world.

You have brought nothing but joy and love into my life. I want to thank you for being a great man to me." Rhema declared.

"There is no need to thank me. A man is supposed to treat his Queen with the utmost respect at all times." I concluded.

After playing a game of scrabble I got on one knee.

"What are you doing?" Rhema asked me.

"You don't know?" I exclaimed.

"I don't." Rhema seemed to be confused.

"Rhema, allow Judah to finish!" Kossi excitedly piped.

"Rhema, I love you with my whole being. Will you marry me?" I uttered, pulling out the jewelry box that held the engagement ring.

"Yes! I will." Rhema jumped for joy.

I am so happy that Rhema accepted my proposal. I thought she would turn me down.

"The ring is beautiful! Good job." Bruno bellowed, shaking my hand.

Made in the USA
Middletown, DE
08 April 2023